The Unity Project

By J. R. Miller

ISBN 978-0-9801487-2-5

Printed in the United States of America

The Unity Project

The Last Christmas

It was a cold snowy night in December of 2074 at the height of the holiday shopping season. The New York City streets were filled with holiday shoppers as thousands of lights glittered against the glass and steel buildings. Children gazed with glee at the holiday window displays with intricate scenes of holidays past.

While the shoppers were enjoying the sights and sounds of Christmas, in a small apartment in the Bay Ridge neighborhood in Brooklyn, a young Muslim man was preparing for his final journey. He performed a ritual bath, put on clean clothes, and set off for his local mosque to attend a communal prayer. Upon arriving he removed his shoes and stepping with his right foot first, he entered the mosque. He assumed the standard position and began his prayer with "Allahu Akbar," Allah is the greatest. Then he continued his prayer, "Glory to you, Allah, and praise by you. Blessed is your name, great is your highness and there is no God except you." Then he repeated the traditional Islamic prayer that is customary before battle, and he asked Allah to forgive his sins, and to bless his mission.

He completed his prayers, left the mosque, and returned to his apartment to complete his final preparations. Back in his dimly lit apartment he put a copy of the Koran in his left breast pocket above his heart, and strapped the nail-laden belt of explosives around his waist. Finally, he put on a black leather coat to conceal his murderous weapon, and was now prepared to die.

He left his apartment and took the subway to Penn Station in the heart of the New York City shopping district. He walked into a crowded department store and began to look around. As he scanned his surroundings the feeling of alienation and rage came rushing back, he saw glitter and gold, stacks of gift wrapped boxes, and Christmas trees adorned with lights, ornaments, and ribbons. The scene reminded him of the decadence, the toxic materialism, and the abundance of the Western world, reinforcing his mission against the twin evils of secularism and modernism.

As he walked toward the center of the store he saw a long line of children with their mothers waiting to meet Santa Claus. He walked up to the end of the line. At the end of the line was a woman holding the hand of her young daughter. The little girl was beaming with anticipation as she patiently waited for her turn to meet with Santa Claus. He asked the young woman, "How long is the wait?"

"We were told it would be about twenty minutes," replied the woman.

The man smiled and said, "Your wait is over." Then suddenly he yelled, "Allahu Akbar!" and pressed the detonator.

The blast leveled the area. Where there was once laughing smiling children, there was now devastation and death. It was a gruesome scene, with hundreds killed and maimed by the initial blast and the nails that had become deadly projectiles. Many others were killed and injured by flying glass and debris. A hand with a wedding ring still intact, lay on the charred seat of a chair.

To the suicide bomber, pressing the detonator is the shortest path to Heaven. It immediately opens the door to paradise. The chances to please Allah, to meet the prophet Muhammad, and to be saved from the agonies of hell, are all strong motivators for the Islamic fanatics. If they can kill Christians or Jews on their journey to paradise, they have accomplished their mission. At the mosque, where the young man had prayed earlier, the followers of Allah danced and chanted in celebration. At the scene of the bombing, the survivors wept in agony.

Shortly after the cowardly act, President Adams received a phone call from the FBI Director informing him of the blast, and what they knew about the attack.

"Mr. President, I am very sorry to inform you that a suicide bomber just murdered over one hundred women and children as they waited in line to see Santa Claus at Macy's department store. The hospitals are overwhelmed by the influx of the wounded. Many of the victims had to be treated on the blood soaked floors and on cafeteria tables."

"That's it! We may as well be living in the Dark Ages. These people are nothing but murderous barbarians. It is time. We are going to completely and permanently remove this scourge from the face of the earth. Let me know when you have additional information," responded the angry President.

The President completed his call to the FBI Director and immediately called Secretary of Defense Robert Coleman.

"Bob, I guess you heard about the department store bombing in New York this evening?"

"Yes Mr. President, I heard."

"Activate The Unity Project."

"Yes Sir, Mr. President, we will begin preparations immediately."

The President hung up the phone. The implementation of The Unity Project had officially begun. The series of events that had led up to the activation of The Unity Project had actually begun in the first years of the new millennium, and would forever change the future of the world.

Islamic Jihad

It appeared to be just another normal Tuesday morning for Diane Cramer and her daughter Melissa. They were up early, had breakfast together, and made their plans for the day.

"Momma, can we go to the American Museum of Natural History today after school?" asked Melissa.

"Sure, that sounds like fun. I will pick you up after school," replied her mother.

Melissa had just finished her morning bowel of cereal and started loading her lunch box with one of her favorite lunches. Her mother had made her a peanut butter and grape jelly sandwich, a bag of potato chips, and an apple.

"Momma, can I have a candy bar for lunch toady, please?" asked Melissa.

"I guess that would be okay. But only if you promise to eat your apple before you eat your candy bar," replied her mother.

"Okay momma, I promise."

Melissa's mother had to move quickly to get her daughter to school and get to her office on time. Diane Cramer worked for a brokerage firm that had offices on the 84th floor of the World Trade Center Tower 2.

Sadly, Melissa's mom did not pick her up after school. She would never see her mother again. Melissa became one of the nearly 3,000 children under the age of eighteen who lost a parent during the September 11, 2001 terrorist attacks.

The morning of September 11, 2001 started like most mornings in the busy city of New York, the mad rush to get to work, the traffic, and the noise. Even with all the normal commotion of the city no one was prepared for the chaos to come. Seemingly out of nowhere an airplane plowed into the North Tower of the World Trade Center in lower Manhattan. Twenty minutes later, a second plane hit the South Tower. Ninety minutes later, the towers collapsed. By the time it was all over more than 2,600 people were dead and thousands more injured, many suffering from terrible burns caused by burning jet fuel. Later that morning, a third plane slammed into the western face of the Pentagon, and a fourth plane crashed in a field in southern Pennsylvania resulting in another 381 deaths. The devastation was a result of 19 young Arab martyrs acting in the name of Allah. The Islamic terrorists, led by Usama Bin Ladin and his al-Qaeda network, had brought their terror war to the shores of America.

The perception that the West is responsible for the exploitation and historical conditions of poverty and external domination of the Arab world has created profound anger towards Western Civilization and its ideas. The United States dominates the world in both economic and military power and the rest of the world doesn't like it. The United States was built on the foundation of an extraordinary constitution, fueled by democratic free market capitalism, and has in 200 years surpassed countries that are centuries older. With domination and success comes hatred and envy.

In the eyes of the Arab world, the history of Arab civilization has been one of repeated defeats at the hands of the West. For the Arabs, the greatest of all defeats occurred when the Western nations collectively imposed the formation of Israel with no apparent concern for the fate of the Palestinians. Arab humiliation intensified as the United States strengthened the Israeli military and armed Middle Eastern dictators during the Cold War in return for their support in the struggle against the Soviet Union. The final intolerable blow came as Arab armies were embarrassed by their swift defeat at the hands of the Israeli military.

The cycle of Arab-Israeli wars continued with the outcome always the same, Israeli victories and Arab defeats. The Arabs desperately needed a victory, any victory that would break the endless cycle of defeats. The perceived victories of Islam over the Shah of Iran in 1979, and the defeat of the Soviet Union in Afghanistan during the same decade, gave the Islamic world a new confidence and hope that Islamic jihad was the solution to the seemingly endless problem of Western domination from which there was no escape.

The Palestinian Islamic Jihad was formed in 1979 with the goals of creating an Islamic Palestinian state and the destruction of Israel through a Jihad. The Muslim holy book, the Koran, contains hundreds of verses, which dictate a holy war or jihad against the non-Muslim infidels. The first battle of the global Islamic jihad is with the Jews. The Muslim faith tells them that God willing they will defeat the Jews. Muslims believe that America stands as a protective shield and the primary financial and moral supporter of Israel. Because of the American role as the protector of Israel, America must be destroyed first, before they can focus on their Jewish enemy.

Islam, as stated in the Koran, has a sacred and mandatory God given duty to spread the Islamic message to all the inhabitants of the world. The ultimate goal is to convert and bring the entire population of the world under the fold of Islam, the only true religion of Allah. Non-Muslims who do not convert must be eliminated. Those who stand in the way must be destroyed. To change this worldview the Koran itself would have to be changed, and you cannot change the word of God.

The Sacred Tablets

It was a hot humid day in the year 2003. For the landscape company worker, it seemed to be just another typical summer day in the Ohio Valley. As he arrived at work the rest of the crew were already loading up the crane truck. He grabbed a hot cup of coffee, went over to the office manager's desk to get his work orders for the day, and then began loading his gear into the truck.

As they left the yard, the worker reviewed the first work order of the day. It simply stated that there were several pieces of granite that needed to be removed from four different schools. He thought it was a bit unusual that four different schools would all need granite removed on the same day, but in his line of work, stranger things have happened.

"What's up for today?" asked the driver.

"Looks like some schools are unloading some old granite," the worker responded.

"Why would they be getting rid of old granite?" asked the driver.

"I'm not sure, but I've seen where companies will take old granite and recycle it into pavers," replied the worker.

"Well I know one thing, granite is mighty heavy, so I hope we can use the crane."

The work crew arrived at the first school where a large crowd of people had gathered to greet them. They parked the truck, got out, and walked over to where the crowd had gathered. While they were trying to figure out what the crowd was up to, two men approached and identified themselves as the school principal and the county Sheriff.

"What's all the commotion?" asked the worker.

"These are protestors. People are very upset about removing the tablets," said the Sheriff.

"Why would anyone get upset about moving some old stones?" asked the worker.

"I guess no one told you. These are not just ordinary stones, these are granite tablets which are engraved with the Ten Commandments," replied the principal.

"Why in the world would anyone want to remove the Ten Commandments?" asked the worker.

"We don't want to remove them. We are being forced to remove them by the ACLU. We were told that if we didn't remove them we would be held in contempt of court," replied the principal.

Meanwhile, some of the protestors had locked arms and were kneeling in prayer in front of the crane, while other protestors surrounded the tablets and locked arms, refusing to make way for the work crew and their crane. The Sheriff's deputies, being good Christians themselves, hesitated to remove the protestors by force. They too, saw no reason to remove the sacred tablets.

As the impasse continued between the workers, the protestors, and the Sheriff, a lawyer from the ACLU arrived. The lawyer approached the Sheriff and demanded to know why the tablets had not yet been removed. He then went on to remind the Sheriff that anyone resisting the removal of the tablets would be held in contempt of court and demanded that the protestors be removed immediately. The only contempt the Sheriff had on his mind was his contempt for the ACLU lawyer. The protestors were the Sheriff's friends and neighbors, and the preacher leading the protests was from his church. Left with the choice of disobeying the judge's order and going to jail, or removing the protestors, he had no choice but to move the protestors away from the tablets. The Sheriff raised is bullhorn and attempted to get the attention of the crowd.

"May I have your attention please," said the Sherriff.

The chatter of the crowd subsided.

"Ladies and gentleman, I am afraid we have no choice but to ask you to disperse and make way for the workers."

Despite some jeers from the crowd, the Sherriff continued.

"Like you, I believe these tablets represent more than just stone, they represent the Judeo-Christian ethic that is the foundation of the laws of this great nation. Unfortunately, we are under a court order to remove the tablets, so please disperse peacefully. We will have to continue this fight in the courts. Thank you for your cooperation."

The worker was a god-fearing man himself, and could not understand why the tablets had to be removed, but he had to complete the work order. It was his job. As the work crew began to remove the Ten Commandments tablets some in the crowd held hands and sang Amazing Grace. Others wept and prayed as the crane scooped up the granite tablets and loaded them into the truck. When the last tablet was loaded on the truck and hauled away, the protestors joined with the deputies, school officials, and the Sheriff in a prayer. This scene was repeated, as one-by-one the tablets were removed from the Cincinnati high schools, first from Peebles, then from Western Union, then North Adams, and finally Manchester High School.

The fight over the display of the Ten Commandments continued throughout the summer. In Montgomery, Alabama, the scene was much the same as it had been at the Cincinnati high schools. Scores of supporters held a weeklong vigil outside the Alabama Judicial Building. As the work crew wheeled away the 5,300 pound granite monument depicting the Ten Commandments from the rotunda, a chorus of demonstrators screamed at the work crew to put it back. A man could be seen shaking his fist in defiance at the workers and yelling, "Get your hands of our sacred tablets, you God haters!"

Alabama Chief Justice Roy Moore, who risked his career to keep the Ten Commandments display in the Alabama Judicial Building, said he would take his fight to the United States Supreme Court. As he stood on the stairs of the Alabama Judicial Building the defiant Judge spoke to his supporters.

"It is a sad day in our country when the moral foundation of our laws and the acknowledgement of God have to be hidden from public view to appease a federal judge. We are fighting a battle. You are all soldiers, even if you don't know it. It's spiritual warfare. If I should fail to do my duty in this case, for fear of giving offense, I would consider myself guilty of treason toward my country, and of an act of disloyalty toward the majesty of heaven, which I revere above all earthly kings."

A year earlier, United States District Judge Myron Thompson had ruled that the monument violates the Constitution's First Amendment, which states that Congress shall make no law respecting an establishment of religion. A judicial ethics panel subsequently suspended Judge Moore for defying Judge Thompson's order to remove the Ten Commandments monument from its public site in the rotunda. The forced removal of religious statuary, monuments and plaques, and the ban on the posting of the Ten Commandments from all public places was well under way.

It had been a very busy decade for the American Civil Liberties Union (ACLU) and the secularists. Working with secular judges the ACLU made major advances in their quest to remove religion from public view and public discourse. The secularists forced school districts to stop distributing bibles to students, banned prayer in schools, attempted to remove the word God from the Pledge of Allegiance, and succeeded in instituting a total ban of school sponsored religious exercises, including the abolishment of prayer and references to God at graduations, football games, and other school sponsored events. In Colorado, a ballot initiative was voted on that would have forcibly removed the tax exemption of churches, mosques, synagogues, and temples.

In the decision to ban the word God from the Pledge of Allegiance, the 9th United States Circuit Court of Appeals said the phrase "one nation under God" amounts to a government endorsement of religion in violation of the separation of church and state. The pledge of allegiance is enthusiastically recited daily by millions of children in schools across America.

As a first step towards the ban of all religious symbols the ACLU forced Los Angeles County to remove a tiny cross from the county seal. The ACLU argued that the Latin cross on the 47-year old seal is a "sectarian religious symbol that represents the beliefs of one segment of the county's diverse population." The cross is a historical symbol, representing the Spanish Franciscan missions that established the first institutions in what is now the state of California. The name Los Angeles is Spanish for The Angels.

Nothing is sacred to the secularists. Secularism rejects all forms of religious faith and worship. The secularists believe in the use of critical reason, factual evidence, and scientific method, rather than faith and mysticism, in seeking solutions to human problems. They believe that the conduct of humans should be guided by considerations derived from the present life, not from the prospect of salvation or the threat of damnation.

It was during the Enlightenment of the 18th Century, with the development of modern science, when philosophers began to openly criticize the authority of the church and engage in free thought. The free thought movement of America and Western Europe made it possible for the common citizen to reject blind faith and superstition without the risk of persecution. The Enlightenment dislodged the ecclesiastical establishment from central control of cultural and intellectual life. By emancipating science from the shackles of theological oppression, the Enlightenment rendered possible the autonomous evolution of modern culture. Many people believe that the general rise of secularism and the corresponding general decline in religion is the inevitable result of the Enlightenment, as people turn towards science and rationalism and away from religion and superstition.

Friction in Europe

The early morning call to prayers resonated from the loudspeakers atop the mosque. As the Muslim faithful gathered for morning prayers there was tension in the air. Paris in 2004 is a vastly different place then it was when the Cathedral of Notre-Dame was completed in 1250 and Catholicism was the dominant religion. Not since the French Revolution began with the storming of the Bastille in 1789 has the country seen such division and turmoil. France's secular culture and the strict division between church and state are being threatened. France has suffered through many of the religious conflicts that have plagued civilizations for centuries and the French are fierce in their protection of the secular tradition.

While the faithful were at morning prayers, Jean-Francois Millet, Professor of History at Ecole Normale Supérieure, was lecturing on the religious history of France and its relation to the current conflict between secularism and religion.

"Powerful religious demons from the past continue to haunt France today. Religious conflict began in France with the Albigensian Crusade in 1209 when the Roman Catholic Church crushed the Cathars. In the town of Beziers, where there was believed to be no more than 500 hundred Cathars, over 10,000 people were slaughtered. The battle cry was 'Kill them all, for the Lord knoweth them that are His.' You may recognize the modern form of this phrase as 'Kill them all, and let God sort them out.' The Cathars that managed to survive the Albigensian Crusade were finished off by the Inquisition. Cathars who refused to recant were hanged, or burnt at the stake."

"Following the Albigensian Crusade was the St. Bartholomew's Day massacre of 1572 where murderous mobs massacred up to 70,000 Huguenots. The Huguenots were French Protestants who were members of the French Reformed communion of the 16th and 17th centuries. In 1598, in an attempt to end the French Wars of Religion the Edict of Nantes was issued. The Edict of Nantes granted French Protestants equal rights with Catholics and succeeded in restoring peace and unity to France. In 1685, the Edict of Nantes was renounced and replaced with the Edict of Fontainebleau, which ordered the destruction of Huguenot churches and the closing of schools. In 1793, a royalist uprising erupted in the French province of Vendee, caused by the murder of King Louis XVI, forced conscription, persecution of Catholics, and excessive taxation. In early 1794, the National Convention decided to exterminate the Vendéens to the last man, woman, and child. In what is considered to be the world's first genocide, the National Convention clearly stated its wishes for the complete destruction of the province: 'Women are reproductive furrows who must be ploughed under.' 'Not one is to be left alive.' 'Only wolves must be left to roam that land.' From this dark past the French Enlightenment evolved, a topic which we will cover in detail in a future lecture."

As the Professor continued his lecture, two young Muslim women were in the student dormitory watching televised coverage of the protests over the proposed ban on religious symbols including the niqab or face veil, and the burqa, a loose garment which covers the whole body except the eyes.

Safia Amajan, a student from Afghanistan, had just celebrated her nineteenth birthday. She was a hard working student and generally did not pay much attention to the news or popular culture. She was raised by strict Muslim parents and considered herself to be very conservative. While growing up in Afghanistan, the Taliban forced all women to wear the burqa.

Safia's roommate Nadia Hussain, was from Pakistan. Safia considered herself to be more modern and westernized. She was always interested in the latest news and popular culture. She wore the veil at home in Pakistan out of fear and peer pressure more than a belief that it is required under the Koran or Islamic law.

"I can't believe the French government is really going to ban religious clothing and symbols," said Safia.

"It does seem extreme," replied Nadia.

"For me, wearing the veil is God's will," said Safia.

"At home my parents insisted I wear the veil but they believe education is more important than strict adherence to Islam. I like the freedom to go without the veil, I feel restricted when I wear it. Even if I don't wear the veil, I have faith that God knows what is truly in my heart," responded Nadia.

"The veil is part of who I am. It's not just a piece of fabric on my head. I don't know what I am going to do," said Safia as she began to cry.

"I'm sure there will be a compromise," said Nadia, as she tried to comfort Safia.

It doesn't appear that compromise in France will come easy. President Nicolas Sarkozy has stated that the veil oppresses women and is not welcome in France. Governments across Europe are banning religious apparel and symbols. They believe that the veils are a divisive symbol, which oppress women and are a potential security threat.

French revolutionaries separated church and state in the 18th century, and the French constitution declares France to be "an indivisible, secular, democratic and social republic." The ideas of French enlightenment thinkers such as Voltaire, Diderot, and Montesquieu who regarded religion as divisive, benighted, and intolerant, are still prevalent today with secularism being the closest thing the French have to a state religion.

The migration of Muslims from Algeria, Tunisia, Morocco, and Senegal that began in the 1950s is larger than any other influx in the history of France. The new immigrants are young and have a higher birth rate than the French. The indigenous French people and the government are concerned that the Muslim population in France could grow from a minority to a majority within the next twenty five years.

Such drastic change requires drastic action. Tranquility must be preserved even it requires harsh measures. Many in France are concerned that their country could become an Islamic republic, an alien world to most of the populace.

The compromise the Muslim women were hoping for never came. In one of their first actions to control the rapid religious changes, the French parliament voted overwhelmingly to ban religious apparel and symbols from public schools. The law stipulates that in schools, symbols and dress that conspicuously show the religious affiliation of students are forbidden. These symbols and dress include Islamic headscarves, Jewish skullcaps, Sikh turbans, and Christian crosses.

Those who violate the new law are subject to punishment ranging from temporary suspension to expulsion. Proselytizing in public schools where the citizens of tomorrow are being educated cannot be allowed. It is feared that proselytizing in public schools would produce even more converts, who would further disrupt the secular state. As with the removal of religious symbols from public schools and buildings in America, the ban has not been well received.

After the ban was approved by parliament, thousands of protestors, some chanting, "The veil is my choice," took to the streets of Paris and other cities in France. The protestors formed a sea of color with many of the women protestors wearing red, white, and blue headscarves, the color of the French flag, as a symbol of defiance. From major European capitals to cities across the Middle East protestors took to the streets to show solidarity with Muslims in France.

As the protests continued, a member of the National Assembly appeared in front of the Palais Bourbon, the seat of the French National Assembly, to speak about the ban and the protestors.

"We are only asking that while in France, people abide by the principles of secularism. These protests against the ban serve no purpose but to encourage tension and anger, and to further divide the nation. One of the basic principles of secularism and the foundation of the French Republic is to make everyone equal. We can see clearly that some can and are being tempted to radicalize things, to twist reality," he said.

The French authorities believe the protests are nothing more than an attempt to stir up racial, ethnic and religious tensions. A French citizen owes allegiance to the nation, not to an ethnic or religious identity.

France is not alone. Only a third of the population in Europe now believes in a personal God. There is growing opposition to the inclusion of any reference to religion in the new European Union Constitution, and there is a growing belief that a need to acknowledge and pay tribute to God is an archaic idea not worthy of modern thought. Although the Europeans are beginning to see religion as a threat to European cultural values and traditions, others see modern Western Europe becoming a spiritual desert, a religious vacuum, given over to secularism and materialism. The long bloody path to European secularism seems likely to continue.

Eastern Dissent

In the early morning mist the flowing forms appeared to be gliding over the surface of the garden. Suddenly, the early morning calm and tranquility was disrupted as two vans roared into the clearing. The rear doors of the vans flung open and four police officers from each van jumped out and ran towards the flowing forms. The officers, wearing their Style-99 deep blue uniforms, pulled out their clubs as they ran towards the forms. As the police got closer to the forms they found a group of seven Falun Gong followers in two staggered lines performing their meditative movements. Before they could flee, the police were on them with flailing clubs. Despite their pleas of innocence and to be left alone, the cult members were beaten into submission and loaded into the vans. Their fate unknown as the vans sped away.

The Falun Gong practices a mixture of Buddhism and qigong or life energy cultivation. This is achieved through meditative exercise that seeks to tap internal spiritual resources. The fervor and the number of the Falun Gong adherents have surprised many of China's communist leaders. The government has identified the Falun Gong as the nucleus of a new opposition group that is using religion to subvert the state, and have accelerated their efforts to eliminate what they consider an evil cult. Tens of thousands of Falun Gong followers have been arrested and many have died in police custody. Many of those arrested are being held in re-education camps where the process of mind cleansing is carried out.

While the roundup of the Falun Gong continued, another religious group was under siege. The next day, in the western Chinese province of Qinghai, a young monk walked through the woods, at one with nature as he listened to the songs of the birds and observed the seemingly endless variety of plants and trees. It was a warm sunny day and the heat from the sun and his long robe had made him hot and thirsty. His journey was nearly complete, so he knew a cool drink of water would soon be available to quench his thirst. As he approached the crest of the hill he could smell smoke. An uneasy feeling came over him as he reached the top of the hill and looked down into the valley. His worst fears had come to pass. There below him was his monastery engulfed in flames. He could see his fellow monks and nuns fleeing from the burning buildings. Not far behind, were soldiers in hot pursuit.

The Chinese government has destroyed thousands of monasteries since the campaign against the Tibetan Buddhists began. The demolitions have left thousands of monks and nuns homeless. Many of the monasteries that remain have become re-education centers for communist party work teams. Refusal to be re-educated on the Chinese version of history, and to denounce the Tibetan spiritual leader, the Dalai Lama, can result in serious consequences.

The children of Tibet are prevented from wearing prayer beads and visiting temples. In school they are taught that the practice of Buddhism is backward behavior and an obstacle to progress. Photographs of the Dalai Lama are barred from being displayed at all public places, including monasteries. It is illegal to own a picture of the Dalai Lama or to possess literature, or audiotapes and videocassettes of his teachings. Buddhist thangkas or religious scrolls, shrines, and incense burners cannot be kept in private homes. Penalties can be severe. For possession of Dalai Lama videocassettes, the offender can spend up to six years in prison.

Later that night, south of China's Jiangsu province, the prayer meeting had come to an end at one of the local Christian house churches and the group members retired for the evening. As the sun came up the next morning the worshipers were awakened by the sound of trucks and bulldozers. Military police and officials from Public Security surrounded the house. The worshippers looked out the window and saw a bulldozer heading for them. They soon realized that the bulldozer was going to destroy their house and them with it, if they didn't get out. In a desperate attempt to get out with their lives they hastily grabbed the children and old people and ran toward the back door. Moments after clearing the back door they could hear the loud crashing and cracking as the bulldozer hit the house. They were too outraged and terrified to rescue their possessions. Now they are destitute, left with nothing, their possessions and home totally destroyed. They join the growing number of worshippers who have been forced out of their homes by the Chinese government. With their home destroyed, they were left with no choice but to reside with relatives in overcrowded conditions, or to live in tents.

The following week, in China's Zhejiang province, another unregistered church building was destroyed. Officials from Public Security and the Religious Affairs Bureau were surprised when they arrived at a church just after 3:30 in the morning only to discover three hundred of the faithful kneeling in prayer inside the church. The authorities shut off the electricity to the building and returned later with two hundred military policemen. The sobbing Christians were dragged from the church and placed in vans for transport to the police station. Once the church had been emptied, the bulldozers moved in. The total destruction of the church was completed in less than one hour. Over the past year, Chinese security forces have destroyed more than 125 unregistered church buildings.

Shortly after the destruction of the church, one of the church leaders, Zhang Rongliang, was taken into custody again, after already serving 12 years in prison where he was repeatedly tortured with electric shocks. He is now serving an additional three year sentence of re-education through labor for subversion. Part of the evidence used against him was words in a prayer journal advocating spiritual warfare to fight atheism.

The Chinese have instituted strict regulations on religious entities and members of religious groups. All religious facilities, their clergy, and their members must be documented and filed with the authorities according to the rules formulated by the governments Religious Affairs Bureau. The countrywide crackdown is part of an ongoing project aimed at illegal and reactionary religious groups that undermine national unity and endanger political and social stability. These illegal and reactionary groups include the Falun Gong, Buddhists, Christians, and other cults and sects.

The regulation of religious groups is used as a means of tracking and controlling religious adherents, including members of Christian house churches. Unregistered house churches organize religious meetings in private homes, and were formed as a way to escape the authority's watchful eye. Secrecy has not spared the house churches. Many members of such groups have been repeatedly harassed, detained, and fined by the police. Harsher punishment, including long terms of imprisonment, and beatings for refusing to acknowledge that they were involved in illegal religious activities is common.

In one incident, two worshipers were severely beaten by the police, and a female member of the group was held by her hair as her head was beaten against a table. They were then forced to put their fingerprints on confessions written by the police. For those who survive the interrogation sessions, they can expect imprisonment, re-education classes, forced labor, or confinement in a mental institution.

In a recent church raid on illegal reactionary Christians, the police removed all of the bibles and religious artifacts. They also confiscated the church's address book, which they later used to visit many of the church members. These visits included harassment and beatings, warnings not to go to the church again, and threats that the worshippers could lose their jobs and pensions if they continued their religious activities.

The Religious Affairs Bureau regulations are broad and strict and include a ban on religious activities in schools and the distribution and possession of unauthorized religious materials. The regulations state that religious activities will not be allowed to infiltrate the schools, nor will anyone be allowed to instill national schismatic ideology and religious creeds into the minds of students. Teaching materials that advocate national division and publicize religious creeds must be resolutely eliminated. Books and magazines must be cleansed of illegal religious ideology. Corrupting the youth of China with religious dogma simply cannot be allowed.

Russia Returns to the Past

It was a busy Tuesday night in August 2004 at the Moscow subway station. A lone woman walked nervously towards the station. When she noticed two police officers standing in front of the entrance she quickly turned around and headed for a nearby department store. As she walked, she noticed a crowd of people standing in front of the department store. She increased her pace and headed for the crowd. As she reached the crowd there was a large explosion, and the woman was gone. Left in her wake was a terrible scene of carnage. Windows were shattered, a car was destroyed and engulfed in flames, bloodied bodies were lying on the sidewalk, and body parts were all over the street. When it was all over, 10 people were dead, and 51 people wounded, many of them in critical condition.

Seven days earlier, two Russian airplanes were blown out of the sky by two Chechen female suicide bombers, killing all of the 90 people aboard the aircraft. In February, forty one people were killed in a rush-hour explosion at the Moscow subway. In October 2002, Muslim terrorists seized 800 people in a Moscow theater. After a three-day standoff, Russian authorities launched a rescue attempt in which all 41 attackers were killed along with 127 hostages who succumbed to a knockout gas used to incapacitate the assailants.

The first day of the new school year is a day of celebration in Russia. School starts on September 1st and is called "The Day of Knowledge." On that day, parents come to school with their children, and balloons and gifts are brought for the teachers. The first day of school is always filled with excitement and nervousness, with both children and parents eagerly anticipating the new school year to come. On this hot and sunny day, filled with anticipation, no one could have imagined the evil that was about to befall the beautiful children of Beslan.

As the children and their parents gathered for school, the al-Qaeda backed Chechen Muslim terrorists were assembling their forces in a nearby forest. Once all the terrorists had arrived they left for Beslan in a truck and two jeeps. They drove into the school compound, where they surrounded more than 1,200 children, parents, and teachers. After the compound's perimeter was secured they moved their weapons and explosives into the school. Once inside, the terrorists forced the hostages into the center of a small gymnasium. The terrorists then attached explosives to the walls and ceilings and placed two larger bombs in the basketball hoops that were on opposite ends of the gymnasium. Having second thoughts, one of the terrorists objected to targeting school children, and was shot dead.

The terrorists displayed terrifying brutality from the start. The group's leader killed two female bombers in front of the hostages by using a remote-control device to detonate explosives attached to their bodies. One of the terrorists held up the corpse of a man who had just been shot in front of the hostages and warned, "If a child utters even a sound, we will kill another one." They didn't let the hostages eat, drink or go to the restroom for three days. The children shed their clothes and drank their own urine in an attempt to survive the brutal heat and lack of water, and endured sleepless nights because they were too frightened to sleep.

As the terrorists were rewiring the explosives, an explosion occurred. Then a second larger explosion occurred, the gymnasium roof collapsed and the hostages began to run. The terrorists fired at them as they ran, prompting Russian Special Forces to attack in an attempt to save the remaining hostages. The depraved terrorists were using children as human shields, and were shooting little children in the back, as they ran for their lives.

When the terrifying ordeal ended over 335 children, parents, and teachers were dead. More than 420 people, including 237 children, were hospitalized, with 58 of them in critical condition. Among the dead were 186 children and 10 members of Russia's Special Forces. A journalist on the scene commented, "When you saw the dead children and their weeping mothers, the sadness one felt was almost unbearable." In a televised address to the nation President Putin said, "What happened was a terrorist act that was inhuman and unprecedented in its cruelty. It is a challenge not to the president, the parliament and the government but a challenge to all of Russia, to all of our people. It is an attack on our nation." British Prime Minister Tony Blair expressed what many were thinking when he said, "It is hard to express my revulsion at the inhumanity of terrorists prepared to put children and their families through such suffering."

The Soviet Union was one of the first modern states to have as an ideological objective the elimination of religion. The communist leaders believed that religion is the mortal enemy of communism and that scientific atheism would supplant what they believed to be mystical religious mythologies, relics from an era of superstition and myth.

Shortly after the 1917 Bolshevik revolution, which brought the communists to power, the Soviets closed seminaries preventing the education and training of new priests, threatening the continuity of the priesthood. The communist leaders confiscated church property, ridiculed religion as mythological superstition, harassed believers and religious leaders, and propagated atheism in schools. The main target of the anti-religious campaign during the 1920s and 1930s was the Russian Orthodox Church, which had the largest number of adherents.

As the Soviets deliberately starved millions in the ruthless battle to impose collective farming on a resistant peasantry, they closed and destroyed churches, arrested priests, and shot many of them based on fabricated charges of sedition. Lenin made the church a scapegoat for the famine, and the government issued a decree to remove church valuables, which were to be used to fund famine relief. He demanded the execution of the clergy, who would be accused of hoarding church wealth as the people starved.

The final wave of repression came during Stalin's political purges, between 1936 and 1938, when the clergy shared the fate of millions of other people the secret police deemed to be politically unreliable. Thousands of priests suffered arrest or execution, and even more churches were closed. Nearly all of its religious leaders, and many of its believers, were shot or sent to labor camps. Conditions in the camps were incredibly harsh. Prisoners received inadequate food rations and insufficient clothing for the unbearable cold. The guards often physically abused inmates. The death rate from exhaustion, starvation, and disease was high. Theological schools were closed, and church publications were prohibited. By 1939, only about 500 of over 50,000 churches remained open.

After the Beslan massacre, there was a growing feeling in Russia that the atheistic days of the old Soviet Union provided more security to the Russian people. President Putin addressed the Russian Cabinet after the September 1, 2004 tragedy at Beslan, "Those who inspire, organize and carry out these acts of terror want the country to disintegrate, the government to collapse, and Russia to be destroyed."

Due to the threat from Islamic separatists and terrorists the Russian government has already curtailed freedoms and has begun a campaign to eliminate Islamic terrorists. Drastic times require drastic measures.

Sacred Land no More

The night of February 24, 1994 at the Goldstein's home was like most Purim day eve nights, there was the traditional celebratory meal, the drinking of wine, and special prayers. Purim is a Jewish holy day commemorating the rescue of the Jews of ancient Persia from a plot by Haman the Agagite to destroy them as described in the Book of Esther.

Earlier that evening, Dr. Baruch Goldstein had gone to the Cave of the Patriarchs to participate in the Purim day services. The Cave of the Patriarchs or as it is known by Muslims the Ibrahimi Mosque, is a series of subterranean caves and rectangular stone enclosures located in the ancient city of Hebron. It is the second holiest site for Jews, and is also venerated by Christians and Muslims, who believe it to be the burial place of the Biblical and Koranic patriarchs and matriarchs: Abraham and Sarah, Isaac and Rebecca, and Jacob and Leah. Jews are restricted to entering by the southwestern side, and limited to the southwestern corridor and the corridors which run between the cenotaphs, while Muslims may only enter by the northeastern side, and are restricted to the remainder of the enclosure.

As he began to pray, the Muslim worshippers on the other side of the partition began to taunt the Jews. He could hear the Arabs screaming "get out of the West Bank" and "slaughter the Jews." Unable to continue his prayers and becoming increasingly distraught he left the complex and returned home.

The next morning, Dr. Goldstein awoke early and put on his captain's uniform he wore as an active duty army reserve doctor. He packed up his gear including his Galil rifle with four 35-round ammunition clips and walked out of his ground floor apartment.

Dr. Goldstein arrived at the Cave of the Patriarchs at around 5:30 AM. He entered the complex through the side entrance. Although the side entrance was guarded by Israeli soldiers, Dr. Goldstein was dressed in his active duty uniform and was well known to soldiers and settlers, so the guards did not challenge him. Once past the guards he moved swiftly to the door of the mosque. Inside the mosque, hundreds of Muslims were reciting their Friday morning prayers in observance of Ramadan, the Muslim month of fasting and prayer.

When he reached the Mosque door the guard said, "You are not allowed to enter the holy mosque."

"I am the duty officer, now get out of my way," Dr. Goldstein responded.

When the guard refused to allow him to pass, Dr. Goldstein hit the guard in the head with the butt of his rifle knocking him to the floor. With the guard disposed of, Dr. Goldstein ran to the main hall where the Muslims were praying.

The Muslims were kneeling in tight rows with their foreheads touching their prayer rugs as they bowed toward Mecca. Dr. Goldstein positioned himself against the back wall, out of view of the video surveillance cameras, and without saying a word put a clip in his rifle, took aim at the worshippers, and opened fire. As the bullets tore into the flesh of the kneeling Muslims, those who were able stampeded for the exits, while the dead and wounded lay on their blood soaked prayer rugs. In less than two minutes 29 Muslims lay dead with another 125 wounded. As the doctor was putting the last clip in his rifle, one of the survivors managed to knock him down with a fire extinguisher and began beating him. The enraged crowd soon joined in, some using metal bars that were part of a partition in the shrine, beating him to death.

For many Jews, Dr. Goldstein was a hero of Israel, but the Israeli government condemned the massacre. Israeli Prime Minister Yitzhak Rabin telephoned PLO leader Yasser Arafat and called the attack a "loathsome, criminal act of murder." Following the massacre, the Israeli government arrested followers of the ultranationalist radical Rabbi Mier Kahane, restricted settlers from entering Arab towns, and demanded that settlers turn in their army issued rifles.

For a doctor, who had pledged to save lives, to commit murder was a surprise to many. Mrs. Goldstein would later recall that Purim day eve was like many before, there was a happy meal, the mood was good, a wonderful atmosphere. She did observe that Dr. Goldstein, a man of few words, had less to say than usual. After dinner, they went for their usual walk with the children. There was nothing special.

Some who knew him could see an escalation in anger and agitation following the 1990 assassination in New York of his hero the radical Rabbi Meir Kahane by an Arab, the land for peace deals with the Palestinians, and what may have been the final act that broke him, the killing of his friend Mordecai Lapid, who died in his arms.

Danger is part of existence in the West Bank and Gaza. Although gunfire is not uncommon, images of settlers firing rifles on the streets of Hebron in broad daylight shocked even supporters of the settlements. Even though there were no deaths in this particular incident, scenes of Israeli soldiers doing nothing to stop the gun toting settlers, with some soldiers even running away, led to the reprimand of several local army commanders.

Fate was not so kind to Talal al-Bakri, a Palestinian vendor who sold vegetables. Mr. al-Bakri, a passenger in a car traveling past the Jewish Settlement of Qiryat Arba in the West Bank, was stopped at gunpoint for no apparent reason at a roadblock set up by local residents. One of the settlers ordered the driver to lower his window. The driver rolled down his window as requested only to get punched in the face and told to turn around and leave the area immediately. Unfortunately, the driver could not leave fast enough as one of the settlers opened fire on the car. One of the bullets hit Mr. al-Bakri in the head killing him instantly, leaving behind a wife, and thirteen children without a father.

Two days later, not far from the spot where Mr. al-Bakri was gunned down, Mordecai Lapid and four of his fifteen children were standing at a bus stop when several Palestinian gunmen opened fire from a passing car, cutting down Mr. Lapid and his eldest son. The eye-for-an-eye vengeance was repeated once again, as the seemingly infinite cycle of revenge and retribution continued.

The settlers blamed the violence on the government of Prime Minister Yitzhak Rabin for negotiating and promoting the Oslo accords and promising to release Palestinian prisoners considered by the settlers to be terrorists. The Oslo Accords provided for the creation of a Palestinian National Authority. The Palestinian Authority would have responsibility for the administration of the territory under its control. The Accords also called for the withdrawal of the Israel Defense Forces from parts of the Gaza Strip and West Bank.

In November 1995, Yigal Amir left his suburban home north of Tel Aviv and boarded a southbound bus heading for Tel Aviv where a large peace rally was to take place. Mr. Amir, a third year law student and Jewish extremist, went to the rally to stop the planned handover of much of the West Bank to Palestinian self-rule. To Mr. Amir, the act of handing over sacred land to enemies of the state was a betrayal of the Jewish people.

Believing he was on a divine mission, Mr. Amir waited for Prime Minister Rabin to walk down from the podium. As Mr. Rabin was leaving the rally he pulled out his pistol and shot him in the chest. Mr. Rabin was rushed to a nearby hospital, where he died on the operating table of blood loss and a punctured lung.

The assassination of Yitzhak Rabin and the increase in settlement violence failed to halt the Israeli government's plans to adhere to the peace accords. As attacks by Israelis against Palestinians increased Israeli Prime Minister Ariel Sharon denounced the attacks as acts of "Jewish terror aimed against innocent Palestinians, out of twisted thinking, aimed at stopping the disengagement."

As the peace initiatives gathered momentum and the violence increased the settlers had been busy constructing barricades, building concrete bunkers, fortifying their homes, and stockpiling food and water. Few could have imagined that the day would actually arrive when Israeli soldiers and police would forcibly remove people from their homes and synagogues. The moment they feared had arrived as thousands of Israeli troops and police entered the settlements to forcibly evict those who had refused to leave voluntarily. In a scene to be repeated throughout the West Bank and Gaza, hundreds of defiant settlers were removed from their homes and places of worship.

In Hebron, Israeli police using sledge hammers, chain saws, and power clippers, entered a building and dragged out hundreds of settlers who had occupied the building illegally. Settlers spit, hurled stones, water, oil, and concrete powder as police, backed by army troops, broke through fortified doors and carried the squatters out one by one.

In the settlement of Morag, troops smashed through a cinderblock barricade, with shields raised and arms locked they formed a human chain to push back a line of settlers. Security forces dragged settlers from the settlement's main synagogue to waiting police buses for transport out of Gaza. Sobbing women covered themselves in prayer shawls and pleaded with soldiers to let them stay. Those who were not immediately captured moved to the synagogue's roof and began screaming at the soldiers "Traitors, Jews don't evict Jews."

"You should be ashamed at what you are doing," screamed a woman pushing a baby stroller.

It was a difficult time for soldier and settler alike. For some of the soldiers, forcibly removing people from their homes proved to be too much as they refused to take part in the operation. Some of the orthodox Jewish soldiers who refused to participate were jailed, while others were court-martialed for refusing to follow orders. The soldiers said the Torah forbids evacuating Jews from the biblical land of Israel.

For the followers of Jewish extremists, it was God who helped create the modern state of Israel, and it is up to the Jews to continue God's work to establish a Jewish theocracy by removing all obstacles, even if that means exterminating Muslims and Jews that stand in the way. For many Israeli government officials, the settlers were fanatics and terrorists bent on rebellion and had to be stopped at all costs.

The settlements have become the latest flashpoint in the war between secular forces and those who promote a Jewish theocracy. Israel's victory in the 1967 Six Day War not only tripled Israel's territory, but the newly conquered areas included the biblical territories of Sinai, Judea, Samaria, and Gaza. For messianic Jews, the victory was a modern miracle of unimaginable proportions, a miracle that indicated the imminent arrival of the Messiah. Redemption was near if only the Jews could control all the biblical land of Israel.

The Jewish people believe they are the chosen people and that passages in Genesis and Deuteronomy provide evidence that the land was given to the Jews in a sacred covenant with God. Relinquishing or dividing any part of the land promised by God to the children of Israel would constitute a breach of the covenant. Secular forces within the Israeli government believe the covenant had to be broken for the survival of the state of Israel, to achieve peace, and finally put an end to centuries of conflict. The sacred land was sacred no more.

The Conflict Spreads

In Palu City, Indonesia, the Reverend Susianti Tinulele started the morning like many before. She picked some fresh flowers from the church garden and placed them in a vase. Flowers have a therapeutic effect and helped her relax while she thought about the sermon for the day. She finished arranging the flowers and prepared to greet the parishioners as they arrived for the morning service.

Once all the parishioners had been seated she took her place at the pulpit and began her sermon.

"We are gathered here today to pray for our lost brothers and sisters, and for our troubled country. There have already been five attacks on our fellow Christians this year. Violence and evil have replaced peace and tranquility. We must do all we can to bring the violence to an end. Together we can make a difference. I have no fear as God is my protector, let us pray."

Suddenly, the silence of the prayer was shattered as five men who were members of one of the retaliation squads, burst through the front door of the Effata church and shot dead Reverend Tinulele and wounded four members of her congregation. When the shooting started, some of the churchgoers frantically got down on the floor, while others attempted to run for safety. The reverend fell straight to the floor after a bullet rammed through her skull. The twenty-nine year old Protestant minister was pronounced dead at the scene. All four of the wounded were teenagers and one of them, an 18-year-old girl, was shot in the left eye, and had only a slim chance of surviving. The gunmen then fled on two motorcycles. Other attacks, including the October 2002 Bali bombings, which killed over 200 people, have been blamed on the al Qaeda linked militant Jemaah Islamiah network.

The period of 1998 to 2004 had been one of unprecedented religious violence spreading like a plague around the world. In Indonesia, at least 1000 people have been killed as a result of Christian-Muslim fighting. Clashes between Christians and Muslims on the eastern Moluccas Islands brought the death toll there to 66 people dead in one week. Thousands of women and children fled their villages to escape the mobs roaming the streets with machetes, spears, and axes. More than 160 people died in religious fighting on the island of Ambon after gangs of Christian and Moslem youths brandishing clubs, knives, and swords attacked each other. Heavily armed police tried to prevent further violence, and police and soldiers had orders to shoot on sight anyone involved in inciting rioting.

In the Balkans, the long history of conflict continued. As the iron hand of Tito and the communists in Yugoslavia crumbled, multiple separatist movements began. The result was a complex series of battles and wars between Christian Serbs and Muslim Albanians characterized by bitter fighting, indiscriminate shelling of cities and towns, ethnic cleansing, systematic mass rape, and genocide.

In the divided city of Mitrovica, mobs of angry Albanians set fire to Serb Orthodox churches and homes as NATO scrambled to deploy up to 1,000 more troops to stifle an explosion of religious and ethnic violence. NATO summoned reinforcements after 31 people were killed and some 500 were injured, in the worst clashes in Kosovo since the allies and the United Nations took control of the province from Serbia in 1999. The new troops reinforced 18,500 peacekeeping troops and 9,000 local and international police. The new troops were attempting to maintain control of the province where Muslim Albanians were demanding independence, and Christian Serbs, many who were forced to reside in enclaves, had to rely on NATO forces for protection. Many of the enclaves are reminiscent of the ghettos of the Second World War. They live behind barbed wire that is protected by troops.

The violence had been planned and organized by ethnic Albanians bent on driving the remaining Serbs from the province. The violence triggered angry protests in Serbia's three main cities, where demonstrators stoned and burned mosques and other Islamic buildings. In one of the burning buildings, several people became trapped, unable to escape as flames engulfed the building. When the police attempted to rescue them they came under repeated gunfire.

In Kano, Nigeria, after two days of rioting, Reverend Andrew Ubah stated that almost 600 people had been killed and 12 churches burned. Witnesses reported that gangs of Muslim youths armed with cutlasses and clubs were hacking and beating Christians to death in reprisal for the slaying of hundreds of Muslims by Christians. A factory worker said he saw two truckloads of bodies being driven along Kano streets and counted at least 30 corpses in the street. Other witnesses reported seeing bodies in the streets, most of them burned, or mutilated with knives. Some of the corpses were burned in wells. No one was spared. Even little children were savagely killed. The bodies of pregnant women were ripped open and their bodies burned. An apparent attempt to make sure they would bear no more Christian children.

The Nigerian authorities consistently under report the number of deaths from religious violence in the belief that the true figures could spark additional reprisal attacks. The government gave security forces the order to shoot rioters on sight in an effort to stop the massacre. The back and forth battles of retribution had been going on for three months before the Kano massacre.

In the African nation of Sudan, more than a million people have been forced from their homes in a bitter conflict over power and resources that also has religious, ethnic, and tribal roots. In a one year period, between fifteen and thirty thousand people had perished in the conflict. It was estimated that an additional 500,000 more will die if they can't go home to their tribal lands, or if more aid didn't arrive soon. These attacks were part of the Islamic government's 20-year campaign against non-Muslims and Black Africans in Sudan. More than 2 million people have died in the fighting. Many of the victims were Christians living in the South.

Since the British partitioning of India in 1947, there has been religious violence between Hindu India and Muslim Pakistan. With estimates of loss of life varying from several hundred thousand to a million, the violent nature of the partition created an atmosphere of mutual hostility and suspicion between India and Pakistan that still exists today.

The violence was not limited to hostilities between India and Pakistan. In 1984, Prime Minister Indira Ghandi ordered the storming of the Sikh's most holy shrine, the Golden Temple complex, where a Sikh leader and his followers had taken refuge. After a twenty-four-hour firefight, the Indian army took control of the temple. According to government sources, 83 army personnel were killed and 249 wounded. The Sikh insurgents causalities were 493 killed and 86 injured. The attack on the holy shrine enraged the Sikh community and shortly after the battle, two Sikh bodyguards assassinated Prime Minister Ghandi. Upon hearing of the assassination, mobs rampaged through the streets of New Dehli and other parts of India for several days, brutally killing an estimated 4,000 Sikhs.

Additional violence followed in 1992. Over 2,000 people died in clashes when Hindu militants tore down the 16th century Babri mosque in Ayodhya. Hindus claim that the mosque had originally been built on the site of a temple marking the birthplace of the Hindu god Rama. The Hindu nationalist movement has been pushing to build a new Hindu temple where the mosque once stood. The most recent violence occurred in February 2002, when a Muslim mob torched a train carrying Hindu pilgrims, wounding 43 people and killing nearly 60, including 25 women and 15 children. Hindu mobs in the Indian state of Gujarat seeking revenge for the train massacre killed more than 1,000 people, most of them Muslims.

The conflict between the Jews and the Muslim Arabs dates back to the 1st century AD, after the Roman subjugation of rebellious Palestine. Acts of terrorism, violence, and killings continue in the region today, especially in the Israeli occupied areas of the Gaza Strip and the West Bank, and in fighting between various religious factions in Lebanon and Beirut. These warring factions include Christians, Muslims, and Jews. Suicide bombings and reprisal killings are a constant part of daily life. Between September 2000 and November 2004 over 1,800 Palestinians and 700 Israelis were killed in sectarian violence.

As the death and destruction from religious violence spread like a prairie fire, the international community began work on a plan to stop the chaos before religious conflict engulfed the world. In the United States, work was already underway on a plan to bring about a permanent end to the violence.

Changes in America 2024

It was a cold December night in Denver, Colorado. There was a damp chill in the air that signaled an impending snow. The Pastor had come home after a long day of activities at the church and had just finished supper. As he sat in his favorite leather chair and relaxed in front of the crackling fire, it reminded him of warm memories of holidays past. He remembered fondly the family gathering at his parent's house, the smell of baking turkey and pumpkin pie as he entered the house on a cold snowy night, and the church choir singing his favorite Christmas Carols. As he drifted into dreamland he was startled when his daughter abruptly burst into the room in an obvious panic, her face contorted by a look of shock, grief, and bewilderment. In her hand she held a letter.

"Father, Father," she cried.

"What is it? What has made you so upset?" asked her father.

"We received this letter from the Department of Revenue. It says that we owe $25,000 in property taxes."

"How can that be, we don't pay taxes?"

"The letter says that religious institutions are no longer tax exempt and that contributions from our parishioners are no longer tax deductible."

"Who would play such a cruel hoax on a person?" asked the Pastor.

"We will have to close the church," cried his daughter.

"Now, now, calm down my dear. I'm sure there must be some mistake. We will go down to the Department of Revenue office in the morning and clear this up."

The move to begin taxation on church revenue and property was no hoax. With local governments receiving the majority of their general revenues from property taxes the lure of taxing church property could not be stopped. The estimated value of this previously untaxed church property was estimated to be over $118 billion. With estimated combined church revenue of $185 billion and assets of $331 billion the additional potential revenue for the government was irresistible. Over the past decade government debt, spending, and budget deficits had risen to unsustainable levels. There was a desperate need to find new sources of revenue to pay for social security, Medicare, national health care, pensions, welfare, and other social programs. Taxes on individuals and corporations had already been raised to the breaking point. Without these new taxes there was a growing fear that the government and the economy would collapse.

Since the taxation of religious institutions began the consequences were swift and devastating. Thousands of small churches, mosques, and synagogues were forced to close. Large churches in big cities were forced to close and sell their property due to the high property taxes on their valuable land holdings. As a result of the new tax laws many religious institutions were forced to merge to become large enough to afford the new taxes. Property taxes coupled with the abolition of the deductible charitable contribution to religious entities had a dramatic effect on the number of religious institutions. Church attendance plummeted, and the connections within the religious community slowly begun to dissolve.

Over the last twenty years much had changed. Many of the familiar sights of the past were now gone. The secular movement had gathered strength and rolled over religion like a great rogue wave. Like France twenty years earlier, there was now a ban on religious dress and symbols in schools. In God we Trust has been removed from coinage and paper money. The word God was removed from the Pledge of Allegiance. There was a ban on the public display of religious symbols and icons. Schools were forbidden to mention religion, religious holidays, and God. The survival of religious institutions was now in jeopardy.

Scientific advances led to a further erosion of the faithful. The discovery of bacteria on Mars, the creation of synthetic life, and advances in molecular biology, astrophysics, and cosmology, confirmed that the evolution of the universe and humans was a natural process. There was no longer a need for a creation event or a supernatural explanation for the evolution of the universe and life.

The archeological discovery in 2015 by paleontologist Otto Benoit that Christianity is nothing more than an adaptation of Zoroastrianism had shattered the faith of millions of Christians. Evidence proving that Jesus Christ was not a real historical person but a mythical creation, that there was massive fraud and plagiarism in many of the early Christian writings, and the realization that it was imitation not revelation that was the source of Christian doctrine, led millions of people to abandon religion in favor of reason and science.

Several years after the Zoroastrianism discovery, scholar's uncovered substantial evidence that the Koran is not one single work that has survived unchanged through the centuries, as the followers of Islam have claimed. The new findings showed that the Koran includes text that was written and edited before and after the time of Muhammad. The idea that the Koran is the literal word of God, unchanging and permanent, is crucial to the foundations of Islam. Without the foundation of the Koran, many Muslims lost faith in a religion that had become increasingly radicalized. The traditional Muslim view holds that God, through the angel Gabriel, revealed the Koran to Muhammad in fragments between 610 and 632 AD. For the true believers, any questioning of the authenticity of the Koranic text as the word of God always results in a hostile reaction, including a fatwa of death.

The evolution from pagan religions to modern religions shows a clear history of the concepts of the virgin birth, the sacrificial death and resurrection, the rites of baptism, the concept of the immortal human soul, and the sacramental communion. Christian and Jewish initiation rites, like the mystery religions, included ceremonial purifications, fasts, baptism, and other ceremonial rites such as circumcision and anointing the forehead with oil in order to be admitted to the community. Nearly every god who mythically died and rose again including, Osiris, Dionysus, Attis, Adonis, and Mithra, was believed to have had the power to give immortal life.

Modern study now concentrated on science, logic, and mathematics. When God or religions were discussed, they were referred to in the same context as ancient Greek mythology. Students were now being taught that religion evolved from primitive concepts and savage rites, including human sacrifice and cannibalism, and that the history of religion is the history of the manufacture of gods by men. A new generation of children had been taught that religion was nothing more than reconstituted mythology.

Although many had traded in their faith for science, not everyone believed the new discoveries to be factual. The few remaining religious adherents believed the claimed discoveries were part of a greater secularist plot to undermine and ultimately to destroy religion.

The downward trend in the number of adherents to religion continued to fall dramatically. The decline had been occurring in all religions and started to accelerate back in 1998, when even the non-theistic religion of Buddhism was suffering from a decline in popularity. The decline was so severe that the Dalai Lama and other Buddhist leaders from across Asia met in Kyoto Japan in an attempt to come up with solutions to halt the dramatic decline. They had hoped that by restoring holy sites in India and Nepal they could give the religion a boost in areas where it once flourished.

The speed and intensity of the secular offensive had caught the religious leaders by surprise and put them at risk of becoming antiquated and irrelevant to the modern world. Many of the surviving religious institutions joined together to fight the new laws on taxation and to counter the secularist's attacks on religion.

After the terrible religious violence of the last forty-eight years, a growing number of people began to see religion as the primary source of conflict in the world and a divisive force that must be eliminated. With the new discoveries about the origins of religion and the advances made by the secular movement, the global movement to remove religion from the face of the earth was increasing in intensity and advancing on many fronts.

The Technocrats Rise to Power

The changes in America didn't end with the rise of secularism and the decline in support for religion. As religious terrorism continued to increase people began to grow weary of the constant threat, and the fear that they may become the next victim of a terrorist act. They were also increasingly agitated with the long lines at security checkpoints, the intrusive body scans and pat-downs, and the disruptions to their daily lives. The American people were not only tired of religious strife and terrorism; they were tired of the existing political order. The nasty divisive politics of the first part of the new millennium alienated many people. People were tired of religious fundamentalism and social issues determining the course of the nation. The old two-party system left people with little choice in what usually came down to selecting the lesser of two evils. High taxes and unemployment, wasteful government spending, corruption, billions of dollars wasted on political campaigns, and the takeover of the government by special interest groups had to be stopped. There was a large and growing chorus of disapproval. The people were demanding a government that worked for the common good, not for political expediency and maneuvering. From this deep dissatisfaction came the seeds of a new political order, the rise of the Unity Party and the Technocrats.

The rise of the Technocrats and the election of Unity Party candidate Robert Adams as President in 2072 represented a major turning point in the political landscape of the United States.

There was a clear mandate that the ideals of the Technocrats were desperately needed if the country was to move forward as a unified nation and remain the global leader in science and technology, and not lose further ground to China, India, and the European Union.

The night of the election, Robert Adams, his wife Elizabeth, and his Campaign Director John Jones were watching the election returns in their suite at the Four Seasons Hotel in Dallas, Texas. With the majority of the states going his way, he was preparing to go down to the ballroom to address his supporters and the nation, when the telephone rang. It was his opponent Jack Reid calling to concede the election and to inform him that he was on his way to give his concession speech. President-elect Adams was scheduled to take the stage to address his supporters immediately following his opponents concession speech.

"Well Robert, it looks like we did it," said John with a sigh of relief.

"It was a long, hard fought campaign, but the difficult task of implementing our plans is just beginning," replied Robert.

"With a solid majority of Technocrats in the Congress we should be able to make good progress," said John.

"The American people deserve nothing less than our best effort," said Robert.

"I am very proud of you Robert. I know you are going to make an outstanding President," added Elizabeth.

They turned off the television, took a deep breath, and made their way down to the hotel ballroom. As the President-elect walked out to the podium, the crowd cheered and applauded. After a few seconds at the podium he began his speech.

"Thank you all very much. Thank you." He paused briefly to allow the crowd to settle down, and then he continued, "First, I would like to thank my wife Elizabeth for all her hard work on my behalf. Without her encouragement and support, I would not be standing here before you tonight. I would like to express my gratitude to my Campaign Director John Jones for managing a well designed and executed campaign strategy. I want to thank the many dedicated volunteers who worked tirelessly to make my quest to become President a reality. I would also like to thank the people who voted for me. I appreciate your faith and trust in me, and I will do everything possible to live up to the high standards you expect and to fulfill the promises of our vision for America."

"In the past, politics has promoted disruptive and negative activities, characterized by demagoguery, factionalism, and inflammatory appeals to communal, ethnic, racial, and religious passions. With the continued terrorist threat, and the increase in global conflict and competition, America can no longer afford the destructive effects of discord and partisan politics. Our highest goal is the security and prosperity of the nation. Policy decisions will be based, and justified, on the grounds of national interests in an increasingly dangerous and competitive world, not on whether the decision will affect the probability of our reelection."

"We offer a new vision for the country. Our priorities include reducing the size of government thereby reducing government spending and waste, declaring war on corruption, streamlining and reducing excessive government regulations, which provide opportunities for corruption and impede business formation and operations, elimination of the insane tax code and implementation of a flat tax, ensuring that America has the finest and strongest military in the world, reforming the political campaign system, and promoting national scientific and engineering excellence. With these changes we see a bright future for America. Thank you again for your support."

Robert Adams was a brilliant man. With doctoral degrees in mathematics and economics from Stanford University, President elect Adams was well prepared for the many challenges that lay ahead. After winning the election by the largest majority in decades, it was clear that the days of the lawyers and professional politicians running the country were finally over.

Exponential growth in science and technology, and rapidly changing geopolitical conditions made it very difficult for people to follow the minutiae of the multitude of issues that faced the country. The number and complexity of issues made it increasingly difficult for anyone but specialists and experts to understand. People began to realize that attempting to stay current with the facts in all the various fields, which may or may not impact their daily lives, was futile. For most people, the best solution was to leave these complex decisions to the experts. The Technocrats, who were secularists, were not influenced by ideology, religion, or politics. The Technocrats based their decisions on the best available evidence, cost-benefit analysis, and whether or not the solution was in the best interest of the nation. There was great hope that reason and science would return the prosperity, tranquility, and security that the people so deeply desired.

Once in power, it didn't take long for President Adams to start delivering on his promises. The Technocrats started showing results within the first one hundred days in office. New anti-corruption laws were passed, a sweeping review of government waste and regulations was begun, work was begun on eliminating and consolidating executive departments, political action committees and tax exempt political organizations were abolished, and political contributions were set at a maximum of $1000.00 for corporations, unions, and individuals, and could only go directly to candidates for office. The increased power and dispersion of the Technocrats was already having the effect of de-politicizing society.

The new government directed action based on rational analysis. These actions were implemented through optimization of the welfare of the people by means of scientific analysis and engineered action. Officials in the new government were chosen according to their technical knowledge not their political connections. They were all experts in their fields devoid of religious beliefs or political affiliations that could interfere with their judgment. Since the new Technocrats were considered the guardians of the public trust they had to be of the highest ethical character and integrity. They had already demonstrated that they were willing to make difficult unpopular decisions that were in the best long-term interests of the nation, rather than surrendering to the demands of special interest groups.

Although rare, and something most people had never seen before from politicians, the new leaders stated what they were going to do, and then they did it. The public was at first unconvinced that the new leaders could really make a difference, but midway through their first term they had already achieved broad public support and were well on their way to fulfilling their promises of totally reengineering government, unifying the nation, and returning the country to its historical position of global leadership.

With the rise of the Technocrats came the continued fall of religion. The numbers of religious adherents were now a small minority in America, Europe, and the Middle and Far East, and almost non-existent in China and Russia. Despite the decline in the number of believers, the terrorist acts that had plagued the world continued unabated. What had been isolated attacks by mostly Islamic terrorists now included Christian and Jewish terrorists, and increased hostilities between Hindus and Muslims in India. In the Southern Hemisphere, there was an increase in sectarian violence between Christians and increased terrorist attacks against Jews. As religion continued its worldwide decline, the fight for survival by the remaining religious fanatics became more virulent.

The Fight Comes to America

The clear blue sky and warm sunshine were a welcome relief after the cold gray days of winter. For the Central Baptist Church of New Jersey, the celebration of the resurrection of Jesus was one of the biggest events of the year. The church members were all decked out in their Easter Sunday best and looking forward to the Easter celebration to come. The children were wide eyed with anticipation of the traditional Easter egg hunt, which was held after Easter services. The parishioners had all settled in as the pastor approached the podium and began to speak.

"Good morning. It is wonderful to see such a fine looking group and to see so many smiling children. Thank you all for coming on this very special day. Let us pray on this Easter morning for the life that never again shall see darkness. God our Father, by raising Christ your Son, you conquered the power of death and opened for us the way to eternal life. Let our celebration today raise us up and renew our lives by the Spirit that is within us. Grant this through our Lord Jesus Christ, your Son, who lives and reigns with you and the Holy Spirit, one God, for ever and ever. Amen."

The pastor paused for a moment and then continued, "Please join me in singing the magnificent Easter hymn, *Christ the Lord is Risen.*"

The church members had just finished singing when a tremendous explosion occurred. As the roof collapsed there was panic as the church members scrambled to get out with their lives. When the dust cleared women and children could be seen crushed beneath the ruble, some of the children still holding a bible in their hands. It was a horrible scene. Blood was splattered all over the walls. Limbs and other body parts were scattered over a wide area.

At first, many thought it was a gas explosion. The thought of a terrorist attack against innocent people worshiping their God on Easter Sunday seemed beyond comprehension. As the investigation continued the evidence began to point to an Islamic terrorist group. A week later, a group called the Islamic Revolutionary Front claimed responsibility for the attack. The perpetrators claimed the attack was in retaliation for church leaders backing Christian and Jewish fighters in the Middle East.

With hate for the perpetrators overcoming their grief, a group of men who lost their families in the explosion could no longer contain their rage. The next day, an angry mob of Christians attacked a mosque. As the worshippers lined up and began to bow to Mecca before morning prayers, the attackers burst into the mosque and started shooting. In a hail of bullets the worshippers were cut down. Those that attempted to flee were shot in the back. The armed mob fled leaving behind more death and destruction. The cycle of death and revenge had begun once again.

A spokesman for the Council on American Islamic Relations stated that they had tallied over 100 anti-Arab incidents since the Central Baptist Church bombing. Shots were fired at a mosque in Texas, and Arab businesses in Indiana. There were several fire bombings and demonstrations in Illinois, and vandalism at Islamic centers from California to Virginia. In Chicago, police had to intervene as an angry mob marched toward a mosque, and in El Paso there were multiple reports of fire bombings at an Arab-American community Center and a mosque. In Alexandria, Virginia, vandals threw bricks through the windows of an Islamic bookstore, and in Alabama several women on their way to worship at the local mosque were harassed and spat upon. The violence forced several mosques to close and those that remained open reported a significant drop in attendance. Muslim leaders were encouraging Arabs to become invisible until the violence subsided.

Because of the escalating violence and tension between the various religious factions there was a harsh crackdown by the government on the remaining religions institutions. A temporary ban on the publication of religious materials such as books, magazines, and signs was instituted, and a ban on religious radio and television advertising and broadcasting was implemented. These new policies were referred to as the out of sight, out of mind (OSOM) program. The government felt that by limiting the exposure of the various groups and their fiery rhetoric, passions could be reduced.

The Summer of Discontent

The summer of 2073 was unusually hot. Both the air temperatures and the heated rhetoric of the discontented were extreme. Protests and demonstrations from both the secularists and the theists increased in frequency as did the level of violence.

Shortly after noon in Detroit, Michigan, there were only a few people walking around in what appeared to be a random motion in front of the One Detroit Center building. Within the span of an hour, the small group had grown, and was now a small crowd. By the end of the second hour the small crowd had swelled in size and now numbered in the hundreds. The crowd that had formed was a group of protestors who were determined to remove the new government restrictions on religion. The protestors had threatened to shutdown city hall and the middle of downtown to protest the taxation of religious organizations and the new curbs on religious freedoms.

As the crowd grew larger and moved closer to city hall, they grew louder and increasingly agitated. When they arrived at the Detroit City Hall they were greeted by what appeared to be several hundred police officers. The police were a menacing site, clad in black uniforms, and wearing body armor and helmets with built-in gas masks. The first row held clear bulletproof shields in front of them and formed a wall around the city hall complex. The second row stood in the ready position forming an inner circle.

When the protestors reached the phalanx, they started yelling and demanded to speak to the mayor. The protestors blamed the mayor for the implementation of property taxes on church property and for the seizure of the Missionary Baptist Church for failure to pay taxes. The mayor didn't appear, but a spokesman for the mayor did. With loudspeaker in hand, he ordered the crowd to disband immediately or they would face arrest. The response from the crowd was rapid and loud.

"You murderer, you have destroyed our churches," yelled one man.

"God will punish you for your evil deeds!" screamed another.

The spokesman's words fell on deaf ears and in an instant, someone in the crowd had thrown a brick at him. A voice from the crowd cried out, "You'll rot in hell!"

As the crowd became more unruly, the police began to push them back. The response from the crowd was to launch a barrage of rocks and bottles at the police. Attempts were made to break through the police line, and the situation began to deteriorate rapidly. The police waded into the crowd with generous amounts of pepper spray, tear gas, and clubs. When the crowd began to fight back, the second line of police began firing rubber bullets at the crowd. The rubber bullets would hit with such force they would knock down a large man. As the rioters were knocked down the police would quickly subdue them with plastic strap handcuffs.

First, the police would put the rioter face down on the ground and apply a knee to middle of their back pinning them down. Then they would bring both arms behind their back, wrap the handcuffs around their wrists, and pull the strap until it was tight. Next, they would bring both legs together, and strap their ankles together. Once the rioter had been secured, they would leave them where they lay, and move on to the next person.

After an hour of fighting, the police through brute force had finally dispersed what was left of the crowd. The streets were full of hog-tied protestors. The air was thick with smoke from fires that had been started by the protestors and by the tear gas used to break up the crowd. As the protestors fled, police buses moved in to pick up the secured rioters. By the end of the day the mayor had declared a state of emergency and imposed a dusk to dawn curfew. As the protests spread to other cities, the Governor dispatched National Guard troops to assist the police in suppressing further protests, help maintain order, and enforce a statewide curfew.

Later that day, at one of the police stations where they were processing protestors who had been arrested, one of the protest leaders was being led up to the Sergeant's desk for processing when he yelled in an agitated voice, "How could you ever understand us, understand our beliefs? You're nothing but a godless heathen!"

"Oh, but I do understand," responded the Sergeant. "You see preacher, when I was a young man, I too was a believer. I had faith. I read the bible. I prayed and went to church. What was my reward? A common criminal killed my best friend. My friend was a good man, who was struck down before his time. When he died, I knew right then and there, there was no God. A benevolent caring God would not have allowed this to happen. The Jewish people were faithful to their God. What was their reward? They were nearly exterminated by Adolph Hitler and the Nazis. There are countless stories of the faithful and the obedient that are needlessly killed. If a God existed, he would not allow the evil, and the death and destruction that we see all around us to continue."

"Man has free will, he creates his own misery. It is all part of God's plan for man," countered the preacher.

"Well preacher, at least you're right about free will. Humans do have the freedom to make choices that are not determined by divine intervention. But free will also means there are consequences for your actions, and the consequences of your actions are that you're going to jail."

The Rise of the Resistance

As the discord and violence began to spread an underground network began to form. At first, the groups were split into disparate factions each with their own unique identity. The radical groups had been preparing for war for many years. They had been paranoid for years that the government and the United Nations were out to get them and take away their freedom. They had been stockpiling supplies, weapons, and ammunition for years in preparation for what they believed would be the inevitable arrival of evil forces.

Other groups included survivalists who had prepared for natural and man made disasters and had plans in place for fires, severe weather, earthquakes, and a breakdown in public services and civil order. Many of these groups had acquired large tracts of land in remote locations where they could survive until their homes and businesses could be rebuilt and public order and services could be restored.

More recently, groups had formed to stop what they saw as a secular attack on the basic foundations of religion. When new laws restricting religious expression and practice were passed, and the tax laws were changed, they began to feel that they were under attack and had to do something to fight back. In the beginning, many felt that letter writing campaigns, protest marches, civil disobedience, and prayer would work. As conditions for religious freedoms continued to deteriorate previously independent groups started to become interconnected. The years of effort to halt the decline of religion had been in vain.

One of the first religious leaders to investigate joining forces to form a common front was Father O'Reilly of the Catholic Archdiocese of Denver. Father O'Reilly, now in his sixties, had been a priest for thirty-nine years. He had wanted to become a priest ever since he was an alter boy in his youth. He came from a religious family. Three of his brothers went into the seminary, only Father O'Reilly stayed to become ordained. He had never doubted his calling. His balding gray hair and wrinkled face showing the signs of the pressures him and the church were facing. The church was hurting, losing people and priests. He had always been a fighter, but through the lenses of his spectacles, the strains of the times were clearly visible in his eyes.

The increase in violence and the growing restrictions on religion were very troubling to him. He knew from his studies of Russian history that the banning of religious materials and the closure of seminaries were the first steps on the path to a total ban on religion. He was not alone. Many saw the ban on public religious expression as the first step towards the extermination of all religious thought. As he pondered the future, the phone rang. It was Reverend Warren of St. John's Episcopal Cathedral.

"Hello Father, this is Reverend Warren," said the voice on the other end of the phone.

"Hello Rev. Warren, I was expecting your call," replied Father O'Reilly.

"Have you talked to the others?" asked Reverend Warren.

"Yes, they have all agreed that it is time. We are scheduled to meet at the Camp St. Malo retreat next Friday."

"Very good, I will see you next week."

In addition to Father O'Reilly and Rev. Warren, the meeting was to include the leaders from the largest congregations remaining in the Denver area including, the Rev. McDonnell of Trinity United Methodist Church, Rabbi Goldstein from the Congregation Emanuel, Pastor Jackson from First Baptist Church, Bishop Stavos from the Greek Orthodox Church, and Imam Abdallah Hassan from the Islamic Center of Ahl-Al-Beit.

The St. Malo Meeting

Father O'Reilly entered the St. Malo retreat off of Colorado Highway 7 and began the drive down the winding entrance. He could smell the fresh pine air as he thought about the many times he had come to St. Malo on sabbatical. The solitude and silence of the mountains had brought a feeling of safety and peace to him many times before. The mountains and the retreat had always provided him a refuge from the burdens of life.

Camp St. Malo and the Chapel on the Rock were situated on 160 acres of pristine mountain land framed against the majestic beauty of Mt. Meeker. It was 1916 when Monsignor Joseph Bosetti observed a falling meteor during the night and in his search for the remnants the next morning he came across a large rock. The beauty of the land inspired the priest and he remembered Jesus' words to Peter: "Upon this rock, I will build my Church."

Father O'Reilly arrived at the Chapel on the Rock, parked his car, and walked over to the Chapel to pray. As he walked past the stained glass window with its depiction of St. Catherine holding the body of Christ on the cross, he could not help but think of the life of Jesus and his sacrifice. He knew more sacrifice would be necessary if the church was going to survive.

The following morning, as Father O'Reilly finished his morning bible study he was thinking about his time with the Catholic Church. As he put a tea kettle on the stove to make some tea, he remembered fondly the majesty of the church with its Gothic architecture, the burning candles with their warm soft glow, the sweet smell of incense, and the tranquility he felt when praying and reading the word of God. All these fond memories were now threatened. Like so many creatures of nature before him, his world was now threatened with extinction. He had prayed for strength in what would surely be a difficult fight. He knew that to survive he would need to combine forces with other religious institutions who were facing the same fate. He also knew that combining forces with what where historically conflicting belief systems could be risky and dangerous, but he had no other choice. It was a risk he was prepared to take. He had just poured a cup of tea when he heard a knock on the door. He went to the door and pulled it open. There was Rev. Warren standing on the front porch.

"Rev. Warren, I'm so glad to see you. How are you?" asked Father O'Reilly.

"It's good to see you again Father. Physically I am fine, but mentally I am very tired. I like you carry a heavy burden," replied Rev. Warren.

"Please come in and have a cup of tea. The others should be here shortly."

Father O'Reilly and Rev. Warren had just sat down for tea when the others arrived. They met them at the door, exchanged pleasantries, and led them to one of the camp's large conference rooms.

As they got situated around the large wooden conference table Father O'Reilly began the meeting, "Gentlemen, thank you for coming. As you know, we are facing grave circumstances. Our very existence as religious entities is at stake. We have seen the deterioration of adherents all over the globe, the atheists and secularists have worked to destroy faith and spirituality and replace it with emotionless robotic thought. We have seen thousands of seminaries and schools close. We have seen our churches, synagogues, mosques, and houses of worship close. These are difficult days for all of us, and I seek your assistance and counsel."

They all agreed with Father O'Reilly's opening remarks and expressed their willingness to do anything they could to help. Father O'Reilly continued, "We would like to begin interfaith protests and acts of civil disobedience as a means of building support for our cause."

"I have heard that there are those who are prepared to begin armed resistance," said Rabbi Goldstein.

"Yes, I have heard these rumors as well. This would be a dangerous precedent, and against the military power of the United States would be very foolish indeed. We must follow the path of Gandhi and Martin Luther King. As Dr. King said, 'the method of nonviolent resistance is the most potent weapon available to oppressed people in their struggle for justice and human dignity,'" said Pastor Jackson.

"Non-violent civil disobedience will show that we want a peaceful solution, but if we can't stop the interfaith violence, the government will destroy us all," said Rev. McDonnell.

"As you know, so far the protests and acts of civil disobedience have only led to increased confrontations with the police, who in turn have reacted with increased brutality," said Bishop Stavos.

"That is true, but the protests have not yet been interfaith actions. Perhaps if they see that the various religions can peacefully coexist, they will end their campaign against us. Regardless, we must keep the pressure on the government to end its war against religion," said Imam Hassan.

"We must all speak to our affiliates and parishioners and convince them that any violence between the faiths will lead to the destruction of all religion," added Rev. Warren.

"It is a pivotal time in history for the great faiths of humankind. I trust in the Holy Spirit. The Spirit is not going to leave the Church. It has not abandoned the church for over 2000 years. It will not abandon us now. Pray for us, and pray for the leadership of the theists. Let us pray," said Father O'Reilly.

There was a moment of silence as each of the religious leaders prayed. They finished making plans for the first coordinated interfaith protests and it was time to end the first meeting. Father O'Reilly ended the meeting by saying, "Thank you all for coming. I look forward to working with you on this just and noble cause."

The meeting ended and the theist leaders returned to their respective communities to work on building support for the interfaith protests. For Bishop Stavos, the battle for the hearts and minds of America was only part of the fight. After the St. Malo meeting he sent a letter to Ecumenical Patriarch Archbishop Milionis informing him of the meeting and the formation of the theist interfaith group to counter the Technocrats destruction of religion. He also warned of increased hostility toward religion throughout North America and Europe, and recommended that he form a similar coalition of religious leaders from Europe and the Middle East to act as a common front against the Technocrats and the global secularist coalition.

Project Definition

While the theists were meeting to discuss a strategy for survival, there was a meeting of a different kind occurring in Washington. The religious tensions around the world, and the increasing anti-government activities of the theists in America had not gone unnoticed at the Department of Science and Technology. A top-secret group within the Department of Science and Technology known as the Department of Religious and Subversive Intelligence (DRSI) had been hard at work. The department's initial purpose was to document and track religious institutions and activities, especially radical religious groups with a propensity for violence. Due to the increased threat and subversive behavior of the theists, the activities at DRSI soon went far beyond simple data collection. Some of the fervently anti-religious members of the department had begun work on a project to eliminate all religious thought.

One of the DRSI team members with a great disdain for religion was computer analyst Kathryn McPherson. Kathryn had lost her closest friend in a suicide bombing in London, and was determined to do something about the continued senseless killing of innocent people.

Late one evening at the DRSI computer simulation laboratory, Kathryn sat patiently staring into her glowing computer screen, watching the computer build a graphical representation of her calculations. She could not help but wonder what the impact of her findings would be. She intuitively felt she knew what the final simulation would look like, and knew that if her models were acted upon, it could lead to global war. Finally, after what seemed like an eternity, the simulation model finished running. The resulting graphs proved her intuition to be correct. Over the long term, the number of deaths from the elimination of religion would be less than the projected number of deaths caused by religious warfare and terrorism. The model also showed that the confiscation and sale of the remaining religious institution's assets, which included art work, artifacts, bank accounts, structures and land, would be more than enough to pay for the project.

Kathryn had grown up believing that people should be left alone to believe and do what ever they wanted, as long as it didn't interfere with other people's rights or harm anyone else. The religious fanatics were clearly hurting others, destroying other peoples property, inciting violence, and indoctrinating a new generation with intolerance and hate. Something had to be done. Now that her results were complete she could finally finish her report and try to get some sleep. It would be a long restless night.

The next day, Kathryn was to meet with Dr. Benjamin Edwards, Chief Technologist at the Department of Science and Technology and Steve Schmidt who was head of the DRSI, to review the findings of her simulation models.

After their meeting they decided they had no choice but to present the report, now known as *The Unity Project*, to the President.

The President did not like the current conditions of chaos and war. The daily reports of the killing of innocent women and children in the name of religion saddened him greatly. As the project team entered the President's office everyone could feel the pressure from the magnitude of the task.

"Good morning, Mr. President," said Dr. Edwards.

"Good morning," the President responded.

"Mr. President, I would like to introduce you to Kathryn McPherson, she is a DRSI project leader and a computer simulation modeling expert and this is Steve Schmidt, Director of DRSI."

The President reached out and shook hands with Kathryn and Steve and asked them to be seated at the conference table.

Dr. Edwards started off by saying, "Mr. President, as you know, while there has been a significant decline in the number of religious adherents, there has been a dramatic global increase in religious fanaticism and violence. This is especially true over the last two years despite all global efforts to stop it."

"Yes, it seems like one day we are making progress in one area and the next day a suicide bomber walks in, blows himself up, and we are right back where we started. If someone is willing to sacrifice their own life for a religious belief, there seems to be little that can be done to stop them from taking the lives of others," responded the President.

As Dr. Edwards handed a copy of the report to the President, he began, "Mr. President, DRSI analysts have been working on various solution options for the last six months. Their findings and recommendations are contained in this report titled *The Unity Project*. The analysis has determined that there are basically two options. Option one, is to continue selectively targeting and killing the terrorists in a war without end. Option two, is to remove the source."

"What do you mean, remove the source?" asked the President.

"Our models show that with the destruction of all religious schools, the destruction of all places of worship, and intense adherent re-education, it will take approximately one generation to cleanse the minds of the masses of religious influence. Religious belief is a learned behavior. Without religious institutions such as seminaries, divinity schools, and theological colleges there will be no place for the training of religious leaders, and without places of worship there will be no place for the brainwashing of the masses," Kathryn explained.

"Is there historical evidence that the destruction of religious institutions can eliminate religious thought?" asked the President.

"History has shown that religious groups and religion can be exterminated. As far back as 70 AD, the Romans destroyed the Second Temple and most of the city of Jerusalem. Without the temple, animal sacrifice came to an end and the Sadducees ceased to exist. In the 1970s, the Khmer Rouge almost eliminated Islam from Cambodia. When they finished only 21 out of 113 imams and 15 percent of the mosques survived. If they would have totally eliminated the remaining imams and mosques, foreign Islamic groups would not have been able to resurrect Islam in Cambodia. Another example is the former Soviet Union under Stalin. Religion was almost erased through a program of executing priests and destroying churches," replied Kathryn.

"The former Soviet Union and the Khmer Rouge were brutal regimes. It is not our intent to execute people for the beliefs," said the President.

"We will use re-education rather than execution. The problem with past attempts to exterminate religion is that they didn't finish the job. Unless all religious institutions and their leadership are destroyed, religion will keep coming back," said Kathryn.

"Without the false teaching of religious supremacy, and the teaching of intolerance and hate, there will be no more suicide bombers, no more reasons to kill people with opposing views, no more war over land considered to be sacred, the cycle of violence will end," Steve added.

"We are already fighting an undeclared war here and abroad. But to expand our cause we will need the support of our allies. I will read your full report tonight and give it some additional thought. I understand the urgency of the situation and will attempt to make a timely decision. Thank you all for your efforts," said the President.

Later that night as the President was having dinner with his wife Elizabeth, he said in a serious tone, "I am going to be required to make a decision that could alter the course of history, change the future of humankind, and change the world for generations to come. Sadly, these changes will come at a very high price."

"Being President is an extremely difficult job, Robert. I am confident that you will make the right decision."

"Do you believe that like the entropy law of thermodynamics, humans are inevitably moving towards a state of disorder?

"Actually Robert, I haven't given that idea a lot of thought. But it certainly seems obvious that disorder has been part of the human experience since the beginning of civilization."

"If disorder is not part of human nature, then we should be able to end it."

"As you know, ending disorder means ending irrational thought and actions based on emotions. This will not come easily."

"No, it will not come easily. But if we are to ever achieve global unification, and put an end to the continuous cycle of conflict, something must be done. Two thousand years of false beliefs must finally come to an end if humans are ever to evolve beyond primitive savages."

"The evolution of human thought has proven to be a slow process for most of the world's population. Many are blind to evidence and fact," said Elizabeth.

The President paused and thought for a minute, then continued, "Just imagine the improvements in the human condition, and the advances for the human species that would be possible, if millions of people turned their minds and energy toward science and technology and away from religious studies," said Robert.

"There are certainly plenty of complex problems requiring solutions," replied Elizabeth.

Elizabeth was a very thoughtful person. For the most part she tried to stay out of policy decisions but she knew this was not an ordinary decision. She understood the difficulties of mass persuasion. Elizabeth had a Masters Degree in History from Yale University so she was well aware of the historical struggle against tyranny, and the history of conflicts based on religious, ethnic, and racial belief systems. She agreed with the goal of world unification and wished the end of global conflict could be achieved, but she was uncomfortable with the means that would be required to implement The Unity Project. She thought back in history to other quests for utopian ideals that were never realized, and did not want her husband's quest to be added to the list. She would support her husband regardless of his decision, for she felt that he was a great man, who was only trying to do what was best for the country, the planet, and for future generations.

It was a long sleepless night for the President. When he was a youth, he regarded religion as a harmless diversion pursued by the uninformed, but after seeing the disastrous effects of religious fanaticism, religion could no longer be considered a harmless diversion. His policy had always been to make quick informed decisions and never look back. This was not an ordinary decision, but something had to be done to prevent the world from slipping into anarchy. The following day the President called Dr. Edwards.

"Dr. Edwards, before I approve The Unity Project and we proceed with implementation, we must first meet with the European Union and the United Nations to build a consensus, and form a coalition for our actions."

"I understand Mr. President, we will await your orders," replied Dr. Edwards.

The EU and UN Declarations

After tentatively approving The Unity Project, the President traveled to Brussels, to meet with the EU leaders. As he left for his meeting, the President dispatched the United States Ambassador to the United Nations to meet with the UN Security Council. They would try to build a broad based coalition to assist with the global implementation of The Unity Project. He knew that China and Russia, with their history of religious suppression and terrorist attacks, would need little persuasion, but he was concerned about support from France and Britain.

At the Security Council the US Ambassador Walter Stevens began by saying, "Gentlemen, today I wish to speak to you about the future of our planet and the future of humankind. Ethnic, racial, religious, and tribal thought is the final barrier to peace and world unification. These artificial barriers and the forces that perpetuate them must be eliminated."

"All of us agree that something needs to be done, and that the root causes of conflict in the world are due to collective thinking and divisive thought. But are we sure that these root causes can be erased?" questioned the German Ambassador.

"As with any major undertaking, we have to ask, is our goal realistically achievable, and does the end justify the means? When we look back at the 20th century, we see that dramatic, and what many thought at the time to be impossible changes, can in fact occur. The demise of the failed system of socialism and rise of global democratic free market capitalism, the fall of the Berlin Wall in 1989, and the collapse of the Soviet Union in 1991, were events most people believed would never happen. The world is a much better and safer place than those dark days of totalitarianism and the threat of global thermonuclear war," explained Ambassador Stevens.

"It does show that incredible changes can occur over relatively short periods of time. It was only seventy-four years between the Bolshevik Revolution of 1917, which brought the communists to power in Russia, and the collapse of the Soviet Union. And, two world wars were fought and won by the allied nations in less than fifty years," said the British Ambassador.

"I am just not sure the world is ready for another global war, even though the number of religious institutions and adherents is now very small," said the French Ambassador.

"We are already engaged in a global war. The elimination of these evil forces is essential if future generations are to be free from a world of hate, turmoil, and war," stressed Ambassador Stevens.

"As you know, we have suffered terribly from the acts of religious terrorists. How can we possibly win a war against a bunch of suicidal fanatics?" asked the Russian Ambassador.

"We kill the fanatics, and convert the believers. With no religious texts, no places of worship, and no religious schools, it will not take long for the masses to forget about religion," responded Ambassador Stevens.

"Changing the minds of men will not be easy," exclaimed the Chinese Ambassador. "We have effectively controlled religion for years but missionaries, and other subversive forces are constantly working to convert the non-believers."

"This is not just a war over religion. It is a war of the individual against the collective, and faith against reason. Re-education will play a critical role and is one of the top priorities of the project," explained Ambassador Stevens.

After completing the debate, reviewing the numbers from the computer simulations, and completing their analysis of the project implementation plan; the Security Council members cast their votes. The vote was unanimous that The Unity Project should proceed immediately.

The UN and the EU had been at the forefront of the movement to reduce the global crisis caused by religious and ethnic violence. After meeting with the US Ambassador the Security Council concluded that religious fanaticism must be extinguished at the source, and that it could no longer afford to keep sending peacekeepers around the globe to act as a buffer against hate.

As part of the agenda of the 127th session of the General Assembly of the United Nations a new UN Declaration to modify Article 18 of the Universal Declaration of Human Rights was issued:

Everyone has the right to free rational thought based on reason, science, and logic. This does not include the right to create myth and legend, to create or establish sects and cults, or to perpetuate mythologies, superstitions, or the supernatural. Any religious or ethnic claims to land, property, or special rights are invalid. Acts of violence based on race, religion, or ethnicity is a direct violation of international law.

Shortly after the UN Declaration, the EU Statement on the Promotion of Understanding, Harmony, and Cooperation was also finalized. It reads as follows:

The European Union believes firmly in the non-existence of race, ethnicity and religion. This fundamental principle is the basis for a conflict free world. The EU is fully committed to the principle that human rights are universal, indivisible, interrelated, and interdependent and that as such they constitute an international standard to which all states should comply. The standards of free market democratic capitalism and the rule of law are the basis for all political economic systems and must be maintained for the universal benefit of humankind.

Strange Alliances

The EU and UN declarations and the effects of the global crackdown on religion had an immediate impact on the world's remaining religious leaders. Many of them had already heard about the declarations and were preparing a response. Religious leaders from the world's major religions had been busy as well. Although their numbers had been greatly diminished, they were not about to let a secularist world crush the last remaining breath of life out of their belief systems.

Many strange alliances have been formed throughout the long history of civilization. Although various groups appear to have little in common, self-interest and self-preservation work in strange ways. Mutual survival often overrides mutual suspicion and hate. With the secularists threatening their very existence, the religious leaders were forced to forget about their contentious past and focus on their future survival.

After being encouraged by Bishop Stavos to build a coalition of religious leaders to counteract the secularist forces, Archbishop Nicholas Milionis, the Ecumenical Patriarch of the Greek Orthodox Church, began the formation of the Council of Elders. Archbishop Milionis, with his long silver hair and flowing beard was a man of great wisdom. He was a respected world leader in the religious community, and had worked for decades trying to bridge the divide between eastern and western Christianity. The 72-year-old Archbishop had a vast knowledge of history and religion with a Masters Degree in History from Cambridge University, and a Doctoral Degree in Philosophy from the University of Athens.

The Archbishop had worked with other religious leaders to determine the basic structure of the council and its founding members. After several secret meetings, the council began to take shape. The Council of Elders would consist of one member from each of the major religious factions and an elected Chairman. The council members would represent the Christian Brotherhood Army (CBA), the Islamic Front Army (IFA), the Hindu Liberation Army (HLA), and the Jewish Freedom Army (JFA). Archbishop Milionis would be the Christian Council member and head of the CBA. Since he was the founder of the Council of Elders and Christians still represented the majority of worldwide believers he was appointed Chairman.

Imam Mustafa Abdullah al-Dulaimi was selected to be the Muslim Council member and head of the IFA. Imam al-Dulaimi is 72 years old with a long graying beard. Imam al-Dulaimi, as the leader of the Muslim Brotherhood, is the worldwide spiritual leader of the Sunni Muslims. He is considered a champion of Islamic fundamentalism, including the spread and implementation of Sharia, and strict adherence to the Koran. Imam al-Dulaimi is a firm believer in Muslim unity and solidarity, and that Sunni-Shi'a unification is imperative for the survival of Islam. He has been active in the export of Islamic revolution throughout the world in an effort to reclaim what he believes to be Islam's manifest destiny. This is to be accomplished by a grand jihad, destroying western civilization from within so that God's true religion, Islam, will be victorious over all religions.

Due to the great divide that exists between Shi'a or Shiite Islam and Sunni Islam, it was difficult for the Muslims to find a representative for the Council of Elders. There are numerous sects even within these groups and their differences are many. They don't even agree on the fundamental aspects of their religion, including the definition of imam. Over the years there have been numerous sectarian attacks from both sides that have killed large numbers of Muslim adherents. Thousands have been killed in Pakistan and Iraq as a result of the schism.

The great schism of Islam arose over the issue of the caliph or the successor of the Prophet Muhammad after his death in 632 AD as the temporal and spiritual head of Islam. The Shi'a, known as the Shiat-Ali or "Partisans of Ali," supported Ali, Muhammad's son-in-law for caliph. They believe the divine line of descent from Muhammad will culminate in the Twelfth Imam, Mohammed al-Mahdi, or "The Guided One." Hidden from usurpers, the Twelfth Imam or so called "Hidden Imam," will appear on the Last Day as the messiah to bring divine justice to the world.

In Shi'a Islam, the imam is fundamental to the theology. The Shi'a imam must be of direct descent of either Hussein or his brother Hasan. The imams are supposed to be divinely appointed, sinless, infallible successors of Muhammad, and provide guidance for the human race in both religious as well as secular matters. Due to this quality, there can only be one imam at a time. The imam is the only one who fully understands all aspects of Islam, and the only one who can give interpretations of the Koran. During the annual mourning of Hussein's death, known as Ashura, the Shi'a faithful march in the streets, beating their chests and crying in sorrow. The extremely devout flagellate themselves with swords and whips.

In Sunni Islam, the term imam is used principally as a title and is the person who performs the congregational prayer. For Sunnis' or followers of the "Way of the Prophet," any worthy man could lead the faithful. The imam is considered the most learned and most respected person in the assembly, and each mosque has their own imam.

The Shiites were the eventual losers in the long violent struggle for mastery, a fact now reflected in their minority status within global Islam. A long history of oppression, beginning with the Ottoman Empire and continuing today in states like Iraq and Saudi Arabia, has led to a strong identification with the injustices suffered by Hussein. Shiites' continue to believe they are the oppressed, and they see the Sunnis' as the oppressors.

Since there could only be one representative for Islam on the council, the Muslim leaders decided that since the majority of the world's Muslims are Sunni that it would be a Sunni leader for the Council with a Shiite as a backup in case the Sunni leader was captured or killed.

Chief Rabbi Elijah Rabinowitz is the Jewish Council member and head of the JFA. Rabbi Rabinowitz is a 68-year-old former captain in the Israeli Defense Forces. He is considered one of the world's most respected rabbis and leading Jewish scholars. He had been teaching at the Mayanot Institute of Jewish Studies in Jerusalem until it was shutdown by the secularist government.

Surya Gupta is the Hindu Council member and head of the HLA. He is one of Hinduism's holiest priests and a revered figure among worshippers in southern India. The 75-year-old priest is the influential head of a sect of India's Hindu Brahmin community. His organization is based in the holy temple town of Knachipurma in the southern Indian state of Tamil Nadu. He is also known as the Shankaracharya of Kanchi. There are five Shankaracharyas or seats of Hinduism in India. The seats are based in the northern, southern, eastern, and western parts of the country.

The Council attempted to include the Catholics but Pope Pius XV refused to align himself with what he considered radical theists. There has been tension and hostilities between Eastern and Western Christendom since the Norman conquest of southern Italy during the 11th and 12th centuries. Even the imminent destruction of all religions could not bring them together.

As far back as the Great Schism of 1378 the Catholics have not had much luck with councils. Pope Pius XV could not accept the idea that the Council of Elders would possess an authority greater than that of the pope himself. He was against war on principle. He believed that if the religious factions could end the violence themselves, there would be no need for war, and a settlement could be reached with the secularists.

The first meeting of the new alliance was to take place in a safe house just outside of Khartoum, the capital city of the Sudan in northern Africa. Khartoum was chosen for its proximity to the leaders, its ease of entry, and for its isolation from Europe and the United States. They had met secretly to determine the structure, function, and rules of the council, and to implement a mechanism to choose new members of the council and their replacements. With the council members in place the first meeting of the Council of Elders was brought to order by Archbishop Milionis.

"As you all know, the satanic secularists are on a crusade to exterminate religious worship and belief. The secularists have been waging a silent war against religion for many years. The war is no longer silent. The stated purpose of the secularists is the extermination of religion. We have no choice but to stand and fight before it is too late."

"Militarily we don't stand a chance against the major powers of the world. Our only hope is to build support among the people, and eliminate the factional warfare and terrorism that are the root cause of the secularist's war," said Surya.

"Guerilla warfare has worked in the past, it will work again. We have many martyrs in our arsenal of believers," countered Mustafa.

"Where will we acquire the supplies, and weapons and ammunition we would need to fight such a war?" asked Surya.

"There are plenty of weapons available on the black market. From small arms to tanks, you name it. If we can come up with the money, we can get the weapons," responded Elijah.

"And supplies of explosives, which are the guerillas weapon of choice, are easily obtained. As we have seen from the past, the infidels don't have the stomach for a long protracted guerila war," added Mustafa.

"We must speak with our traditional wealthy supporters, and acquire the funds we need to purchase fuel, supplies, food and medicine, and weapons and ammunition. Without these essentials we will be unable to fight a prolonged battle," said Nicholas.

"I know of a merchant we can contact about weapons and ammunition," said Elijah.

"I know where we can obtain medical supplies," said Surya.

"I will work on obtaining explosives and preparing our sacred bombers," said Mustafa.

"With holy lance in hand, we will annihilate the agents of evil, and by the grace of God we shall prevail," exclaimed Nicholas.

"The atheists are robots, devoid of emotions and feelings, it will not be an easy fight," said Mustafa.

"They have left us no choice. The godless ones must be defeated. We have much to do. We will meet again in two weeks in Alexandria, Egypt," said Nicholas.

The Reception

President Adams was very grateful for the support of the allies and wanted to thank them personally. He knew that without their support, The Unity Project would be difficult if not impossible to implement. He was especially grateful to the British government for their long-term unwavering support for the United States. He talked with Elizabeth about having a reception for the British at the White House to show his gratitude for their support.

"Elizabeth, I would like to have a reception for some of our key allies for their support in the fight against the terrorists. If I give you a list of guests, could you speak with the staff about the preparations?"

"Yes Robert, I would be a happy to take care of it. We haven't had a party around here since you took office."

The President continued, "I wanted to see if we could get Dr. Goldman, the astrophysicist to come as well. I would love to talk to him about quantum gravity."

"I will certainly try, but if he can't make it, you will just have to talk to me instead."

The First Lady enjoyed parties and socializing. It gave her a chance to meet new people and build support for her own causes, of which she had many. With the prospects of war becoming closer to reality, this would most likely be the last party for quite some time. It would give the President a rare chance to relax and enjoy some intellectual conversation with the heads of state and noted scientists that were to be among the invited guests. Ordinarily, the President wasn't fond of parties, but they were very useful for meeting dignitaries and building international alliances.

The night of the reception had finally arrived. The reception was being held in the East Room of the White House. The East Room is traditionally used for large gatherings, such as dances, award presentations, concerts, and bill-signing ceremonies. The East Room retains the late 18th century classical style with its Fontainebleau parquet oak floor, its white paneled walls and decorative plaster ceiling, and its three magnificent Bohemian cut-glass chandeliers. The tables were all decorated with white tulips and roses, and the room shimmered with sophistication.

The President and First Lady were greeting the guests as they arrived. Among the dignitaries were Nigel Barnett, Undersecretary of the British Foreign Office and his colleague Angela Kibble, who was the Director of Strategy and Information. They would play a key role in developing the strategy for the implementation of The Unity Project in Europe.

Angela was from a wealthy British family and attended the exclusive Cheltenham Ladies College until coming to the United States to attend Harvard University. After graduating from Harvard with a degree in Political Science she returned to Britain and attended Oxford University Law School. Angela liked to party, but being in a high level government position, she had to keep a low profile, and with the travel and long hours required by her work, there was rarely time for play.

After moving through the reception line, Nigel and Angela finally reached the President. Undersecretary Barnett introduced himself and Angela to a captivated President and the First Lady.

Angela was stunning and sophisticated with her auburn-blonde hair, sparkling green eyes, vibrant smile, and a walk that was part catwalk model, part debutante queen. Heads would turn whenever she entered a room. Her long silky hair was tied up in an elegant bun, her form fitting full-length pearl satin gown following her well shaped figure to the floor. With her gold pearl earrings and pearl necklace she was absolutely radiant, and looked more like royalty than a visiting diplomat.

"Mr. President, Nigel Barnett, Undersecretary of the British Foreign Office, and this is Angela Kibble our Director of Strategy and Information, she will be working with you and the Secretary of State on the new project."

Angela offered her hand and said, "It is an honor to meet you Mr. President. I look forward to working with you." Even though she was eager to speak to the President, she dared not linger and moved on quickly to greet the First Lady. "It is a pleasure to meet you Mrs. Adams, thank you so much for inviting us to your reception."

"It is a pleasure to meet you as well. Thank you for your support of America, and the President's policies," replied Mrs. Adams.

As the Undersecretary and Angela continued down the reception line, Mrs. Adams remarked to the President, "Ms. Kibble is not what I expected for a bureaucrat from the Foreign Office." The President nodded in agreement.

The President and First Lady finished receiving the guests and sat down for dinner. The guests dined on avocado and heirloom tomato salad with toasted cumin dressing, grilled halibut, bay scallop risotto and lobster sauce, roasted rack of lamb, wild mushrooms and Armagnac sauce, sweet potato flan, and autumn vegetables. For desert the guests were treated to Arabica ice cream and coffee liquor parfait, with caramelized banana and pineapple. The evening ended with a performance by the Bach Society String Quartet playing Bach's Violin Concerto in E major. By all accounts a splendid time had by all.

The Plans of War

Dr. Edwards arrived at the gate of the Department of Science and Technology and handed his ID card to the guard. The guard scanned his ID card. The security system verified his credentials, and recorded the date and time of his arrival at the facility. Once cleared, the guard opened the gate and Dr. Edwards proceeded to the parking area. As he walked to the main entrance he was thinking about lasers and particle beams, and how they could be used in the fight against global terrorism. He arrived at the main entrance swiped his ID card and placed his hand on the biometric reader. The sliding stainless steel door opened and he entered the secure operations center. He then headed down the long hall to the computer simulation laboratory. He entered the lab and found Kathryn at her usual position in front of the computer screen.

"Kathryn, I need to speak with you and Steve," he said in a solemn tone. By the tone in his voice, Kathryn knew that The Unity Project had been approved.

"I have a feeling we're going to be working a lot of overtime around here," she said.

They left the simulation center and walked over to Steve's office. They arrived at Steve's office to find him with a blank stare on his face peering into his flat panel display.

"Steve, I have just finished meeting with the President. He has met with the EU leaders and Ambassador Stevens has met with the UN Security Council. The Unity Project has been approved.

I'm going to arrange a meeting with the Secretary of Defense, the Joint Chiefs, and the National Security Director for next Tuesday morning at 9:00 AM. We will need to have the tasks and resources, the project timeline, and the final intelligence report completed before the meeting," said Dr. Edwards."

"No problem. We'll be ready," said Steve.

"I will see you next week," said Dr. Edwards.

The following week members of the President's National Security team met at the Pentagon. Attending the meeting was National Security Director Richard Foster and his staff, Secretary of Defense Robert Coleman, Chairman of the Joint Chiefs of Staff General Jason Tillman and his staff, and Dr. Edwards from the Department of Science and Technology and his team from DRSI.

Robert Coleman, the Secretary of Defense, started the meeting, "The President has tentatively approved The Unity Project and is now waiting for this group to complete the final plans of the project before activation."

"The Unity Project consists of two major sub-projects. One is the domestic project code named Operation New Dawn; the other is the international project, code named Operation Unity. Today, we are going to do a strategic overview of the war plans for Operation Unity, followed by a brief overview of Operation New Dawn."

"As you know, we have been faced with terrorist attacks in many of the rogue countries in northern Africa and the Islamic Front Nations (IFN), which includes Saudi Arabia, Iran, Yemen, Iraq, Jordan, Libya, and the United Arab Emirates. Terrorists have been using bases in Iran, Yemen, and Syria to launch attacks against American targets and our allies. Our overall strategy is for allied forces to move south towards the Islamic Front Nations, while at the same time initiate an assault to the north from the Arabian Sea in a pincer movement."

A pincer movement or double envelopment leads to the attacking army facing the enemy in front, on both flanks, and in the rear. If the attacking pincers link up in the enemy's rear, the enemy is encircled.

"We have been working with the UN Security Council and the EU to form an alliance for the implementation of The Unity Project. The North Atlantic Treaty Organization has been preparing tactical battle plans for each of the primary fields of operation. In Phase I of the plan, Russia will be moving south and take control of Georgia, Ukraine, Kazakhstan, Uzbekistan, and Turkmenistan. China, India, and Japan will move south and take control of Indonesia and Malaysia. Japan will also be assisting the Philippines in exterminating pockets of Islamic and Christian radicals. Once these areas have been secured, NATO forces will move in and begin cleansing and re-education operations. In the Southern Hemisphere, which will be the last stage of the war, we are working with Columbia and Brazil to define target areas and re-education plans, and in Africa, we will move into Algeria, Sudan, and Somalia once the Islamic Front Nations have been secured. General Tillman will now provide a brief tactical overview."

"Initially, the main focus for US forces will be Turkey. It is of the highest strategic importance. It is the bridge between the two cultures of Europe and the Arab world, and is critical to the success of the war. Once Turkey is secured we will be ready for Phase II, which will be a major assault against North Africa, Saudi Arabia, Iraq, and Iran. Special Forces units are already on the ground in Turkey and are performing reconnaissance missions."

"The final assault against the Islamic Front states will begin with heavy air assaults utilizing cruise missiles and drones. Once the command and control infrastructure has been destroyed, we will initiate the amphibious landing from the Arabian Sea and push rapidly to the north. Once ground control has been established, the Contraband Eradication and Structural Demolition Units will move in to complete the mission."

"We will be following the doctrine of rapid dominance. We will rapidly reduce the adversary's understanding, ability, and will to respond to an attack, thereby rendering them impotent. We will be using the standard methods to induce the psychological effects desired by rapid dominance. This will include the use of direct force applied to command and control centers, overwhelming combat force, rapidity of action, selective denial of information, and broad spectrum dissemination of disinformation."

"In the first attack, we will be striking command and control facilities that manage air-defense systems. Once all air-defense systems have been destroyed, we will have safe uncontested airspace for our pilots and drones as we move into the full-scale offensive phase. This first attack will be followed immediately by a second wave of attacks, which will destroy the remaining command and control, communications, and military and police headquarters facilities. This will be followed by airborne assaults by US Special Operations Forces, which will secure missile launch facilities, command-and-control facilities, power and water plants, and all media outlets including newspapers, Internet, and radio and television broadcasting facilities. Once these sites are secure, ground forces will move in to cleanup any remaining regular troops or insurgents. Following ground force cleanup operations, CESDUs will move in and perform final cleansing operations. Dr. Edwards will now provide a brief overview of cleansing and re-education operations."

At this point, Dr. Edwards began describing the cleansing operations, "CESDUs accompanied by ground forces will then move in immediately to destroy all religious structures, capture religious schools for conversion to re-education camps, and destroy all religious texts, symbols, and monuments. Simultaneously, we will take control of the radio and television facilities and begin broadcasting the message of reason."

Dr. Edwards continued, "Since we will be destroying all religious structures, there will not be any facilities available for the assembly of large groups for the purpose of agitation and coordination."

"Once we have secured the food distribution facilities, and water and electrical plants, the allied forces will have control over the civilian populations. If the civilians don't cooperate they will get restricted amounts of food, water, and electricity. This control could also be used as a coercive mechanism to force civilians to identify insurgents and to develop an informant network. All civilians that cooperate will be rewarded, and given assurances of anonymity and security," added Steve Schmidt.

"The rules of engagement are clear. We have to remember that our primary targets are not civilians they are terrorists and theist forces. We must keep collateral damage to a minimum or it will only serve to further alienate the population. The destruction of religious structures is to take place only after verification that the structure is empty and there are no civilians in close proximity," said General Tillman.

After the military presentation was complete, National Security Director Foster presented a quick review of the key people and groups that comprised the theist enemies.

"Intelligence sources have put together profiles on the main organized groups of resistance. These include the Christian Brotherhood Army (CBA), the Islamic Front Army (IFA), the Hindu Liberation Army (HLA), and the Jewish Freedom Army (JFA). These groups are loosely coordinated through a group of four religious leaders known as the Council of Elders. The Council of Elders generally meets on a bi-weekly basis and the council members are constantly moving to avoid being captured or killed. Details of the Council of Elders organization and profiles of its members are included in your reports," said National Security Director Foster.

"What about the Buddhists?" Kathryn asked.

"We do not consider Buddhism to be a religion. We consider Buddhism to be an Eastern philosophy similar to Taoism. Buddhist philosophy is fundamentally non-violent. Many Buddhists have refused to take up arms under any circumstances, even knowing that they would be killed as a result. The Buddhist code permits them to defend themselves, but it forbids them to kill, even in self-defense," replied Director Foster.

Dr. Edwards then told the story about a Buddhist monk who was asked, "If someone had wiped out all the Buddhists on earth and you were the last one left, would you not try to kill the person who was trying to kill you, and in so doing save Buddhism?" His response, "If there is any truth to Buddhism and the Dharma, it will not disappear from the face of the earth, but will reappear when seekers of truth are ready to rediscover it. In killing, I would be betraying and abandoning the very teachings I would be seeking to preserve."

"Although there are a few examples of Buddhists engaging in violence and even war, such as in the 14th century, when Buddhist fighters led the uprising that evicted the Mongols from China, and Buddhist support for the civil war in Sri Lanka between the Buddhist Sinhalese majority and the Hindu Tamil minority, we don't currently see them as a threat to peace and stability," said General Tillman.

"Dr. Edwards will now give us a brief overview of Operation New Dawn," said Defense Secretary Coleman.

"Yes, thank you. The plans for Operation New Dawn are nearly complete. DRSI has identified all religious targets in the United States and Canada and has forwarded them to the army. CESDUs will be starting in the Midwest and on both the east and west coasts. The first and largest re-education camp, Camp Enlightenment is already operational. Educational materials have already been printed, and the Public Broadcasting System is ready to start broadcasting New Dawn educational programming. Priority targets have been identified and as soon as the President gives the word we are ready to begin operations," said Dr. Edwards.

"When will the armed forces be ready to go?" asked National Security Director Foster.

"Several key combat units have already been moved to the Middle East and the remaining units are being readied for deployment to the region. We will be using a relatively small contingent of ground troops backed up by massive use of air power and precision-guided munitions. As soon as the President gives the go-ahead for the invasion, we're ready to go," said Defense Secretary Coleman.

"I think we have covered all possible aberrations and contingencies, and the plan looks solid. Our calculations show that the probability of success within the desired time frame is 95 percent," said Dr. Edwards.

"Thank you all for your efforts and hard work. If everyone is in agreement, I will send a final draft of the war plan to the President," said Defense Secretary Coleman.

Everyone appeared satisfied with the plans, so the meeting ended and the war plans were sent to the President for his approval.

The Battle Begins

It was now March 2074, and the President, along with most residents of the northeast, was looking forward to spring and some warmer weather. President Adams was completing his final review of the war plans and thinking about the critical success factors for the Unity Project. He knew that the coalition must eliminate any chance of the theists gaining political or broad popular support, that violence and acts of terror must come to an end immediately after combat operations were complete, that there could be no large scale resistance or guerilla warfare, that the destruction of religious institutions and structures, and religious books and icons, must be discrete and swift, and that the masses have to see a rapid improvement in their daily lives.

He was not worried about the military aspects of the war. The United States and its allies had overwhelming military superiority. The real difficulties would begin after the military action ended. Convincing the populations of the defeated countries that it was in their best long-term interest to forget about religious, ethnic, and racial divisions was going to be the biggest challenge of the Unity Project. Even though groups that defined themselves by a religious, ethnic, or racial identity were a minority, they were nonetheless a vocal minority. As he was thinking about the re-education phase of the project, the phone rang. It was the FBI Director calling to inform him about the New York City department store bombing. The Unity Project was activated.

For the United States the battle started at home. The war plans included a plan for the systematic destruction of all religious institutions and religious texts. DRSI had provided the army with the locations of all the remaining religious institutions and suspected sites where religious texts were housed. DRSI had also compiled lists of all the members of the remaining churches, mosques, synagogues, and temples, and would eventually visit them all to make sure they were not in possession of religious contraband. There was a detailed listing of all religious bookstores and religious supply companies that were targeted for either destruction or confiscation. The war plan included provisions for the conversion of the larger seminaries into state universities of science and technology, and religious camps and retreats into New Dawn re-education camps. It didn't take long for the cleansing process to begin.

In order to carry out its mission the Army had developed new special units to facilitate the implementation of The Unity Project. The new Army units were called Contraband Eradication and Structural Demolition Units (CESDUs). The CESDUs consisted of two Armored Personnel Carriers (APCs) each with five armed soldiers, a large Caterpillar wheel loader, a dump truck, and a Flamethrower Support Vehicle (FSV) with a driver and armed soldier in the cab and two Fire Control Technicians (FCTs) in the rear of the truck. The soldiers of the CESDUs wore a special symbol on their uniforms and were armed with automatic rifles with under barrel grenade launchers. The symbol was a circle with two swords overlaid on top of the circle forming an x-shape. The FCTs were responsible for the operation and maintenance of the flamethrowers and fire containment. The CESDU's mission was to destroy religious contraband and religious icons and texts, and religious structures such as churches, mosques, synagogues, and temples.

Because of people's instinctive fear of fire, the flamethrower can have a dramatic psychological impact. Even the flamethrower gunner is a little afraid of his weapon. The basic idea of the flamethrower is to spread fire by launching a burning fuel. During the Byzantine Empire 'Greek fire' was used as a weapon. Greek fire was a mixture that created a highly flammable oil-based fluid and was pumped out of narrow brass tubes. It was used as a mounted weapon on ships and on the walls of Constantinople.

Modern handheld flamethrowers consist of a backpack with three cylinder tanks. The two outside tanks hold a flammable, oil based, liquid fuel. The middle tank holds a flammable compressed gas such as butane. The compressed gas provides the pressure to drive the liquid fuel through a hose, which is connected to the gun. Pulling the trigger on the gun opens a valve allowing the pressurized fuel to flow through the nozzle. An ignition system creates a small flame in the front of the nozzle, which ignites the flowing fuel, creating the fire stream. A flamethrower can shoot a burning fuel stream as far as 150 feet.

The First Baptist Church had been part of the landscape in Little Rock, Arkansas, for generations, and was one of the last remaining Baptist churches in the area. Many of townspeople's great grandparents had been baptized, married, and buried there. It was dusk when the army CESDU arrived at the edge of the church grounds. Inside the church, the preacher had just finished his supper prayer when he heard the rumble of heavy vehicles and ran out to see what all the commotion was about. There before him was a group of menacing looking military vehicles.

"What are you doing here? What is it that you want?" asked the preacher.

From one of the armored personal carriers a voice crackled over a loudspeaker, "We have orders to confiscate all salvageable church property and to demolish this structure."

"There must be some mistake. I have done nothing wrong. You cannot destroy my church!" pleaded the preacher.

"There is no mistake. We have our orders. Please move away from the structure," the voice commanded.

"No, I won't let you, I am a servant of God and this is his house."

"You have ten seconds to obey, or we will be forced to physically remove you."

The preacher began to pray. Then he turned and ran back into the church.

The loudspeaker crackled to life once more, "You must surrender immediately or your safety cannot be guaranteed."

As they waited the Sergeant said to his men, "We'll give him one minute to think about it, and then we will have to go in."

Suddenly, the front door of the church flew open and the preacher came running out firing his shotgun at the soldiers screaming, "I will only surrender to God!"

The soldiers had no choice but to return fire, killing the preacher instantly. The dead preacher lay on the ground as the demolition crew drove by his body to clean out and destroy the church.

"That was quite irrational Sir," said one of the soldiers to the Sergeant in charge.

As the Sergeant shook his head he said, "Yes it was. Bag him, and let's get to work."

They put the preacher's body into a body bag and threw him into the back of the truck. The crew then removed all the bibles and valuables from the church. They placed the valuables in the FSV and put the bibles in a pile in front of the church. One of the soldiers walked up to the pile, ignited his flamethrower, and turned the books to ashes.

The time had come for the wheel loader to begin its work. The driver backed the wheel loader off the trailer and began to dig a large hole next to the church. When the hole was finished he headed for the church. Slamming into each corner of the church, the structure came down quickly. The debris from the structure was pushed into the hole and covered with dirt.

When the CESDU unit had completed its work, a vacant lot was all that was left. The governments 'out of sight out of mind' policy applied to structures as well. No one driving by the site would have ever known that the previous day a church stood on the property. The CESDU crews preferred to use wheel loaders to level structures, and tried to avoid large fires as much as possible in order to limit unnecessary attention to their activities.

Later that week, in Springfield, Missouri, a producer of religious contraband had been targeted. The Springfield Church Supply Company was one of the largest producers of bibles and church supplies in the Midwest. The CESDU arrived just as the plant was closing for the weekend.

The CESDU moved in with one APC taking position in the front of the building, while the second APC, the FSV and the dump truck, took up positions in the rear of the building. The rear of the building was secured to prevent anyone from fleeing with the contraband, and to prepare for the destruction of the contraband. The unit leader and four soldiers got out of the APC and entered the front of building. The receptionist and the owner were in the front of the building when the soldiers came in. The unit leader walked up to the owner and handed him a document explaining the seizure of his property and the compensation he was to receive.

"By order of the federal government and its power of eminent domain, this property now belongs to the United States government," said the Sergeant in charge of the CESDU team.

The power of eminent domain was recognized by the Supreme Court as necessary to the existence of the national government. The Fifth Amendment to the Constitution states, 'nor shall private property be taken for public use, without just compensation.' The seizure of the church supply business met both the criteria. The building was going to be for public use, and the owner would be compensated.

"My business is not for sale," replied the business owner.

"We are not buying, we are seizing. You and the young lady will have to leave the premises immediately."

"I won't leave. You can't do this. I am calling the police!"

"I'm sorry Sir, we have our orders. You will leave peacefully, or we will be forced to physically remove you. It's your choice."

Obviously outnumbered and outgunned the owner and the receptionist left without incident. On his way out the front door the owner turned and said, "My attorney will be contacting your superiors."

"Fine Sir, but do not attempt to return to this property or you will be arrested."

The soldiers then performed a sweep of the building to make sure it was empty. They opened the back loading dock door and backed the dump truck up to the loading dock. One of the soldiers started up a forklift and began loading pallets of bibles and church supplies into the back of the dump truck. When it was full, the truck was driven to the center of the parking lot where the load was dumped. The truck would then return to the dock door for another load. This continued until all the contraband and books had been removed from the warehouse and dumped in the parking lot.

Once the building had been cleared of contraband, it was time for the FCTs to swing into action. The two FCTs stood side-by-side and torched the pile of contraband and books. With the help of the flamethrowers, the pile burned quickly. With the contents reduced to ashes, the soldiers put new locks on the doors and departed.

The systematic destruction of religious icons and structures, and the burning of religious books had begun in earnest. Scenes of the destruction of religious objects and their support structures would continue until there were none left.

The Guerilla War

Word of the preacher's death by army troops traveled fast. The killing of the preacher was like throwing gasoline on a fire, fueling the anger and hate of the theists towards the Technocrats. The fact that the soldiers killed the preacher in self-defense made no difference. When word got out that the government had already begun the systematic destruction of religious structures, the resistance movement began its attacks.

The resistance in America had been growing, but most people were very hesitant about taking up arms against the government. Jack Cody was not one of those people. After the killing of the preacher, he claimed that he had heard directly from God, and God told him that he must become the avenging angel. Through his hand, the satanic forces of evil that were the secularists must be stopped.

Christian extremist groups began to form in the United States during the Clinton administration after the botched FBI assault on a Protestant sect at Waco Texas, where 76 people including 20 children and two pregnant women were killed, and the killing of Vicki Weaver while she held her baby in arms by an FBI sniper at Ruby Ridge. After the Waco siege and the Ruby Ridge incident, distrust and hatred of the federal government increased dramatically leading to the tragic bombing of the Murrah Federal Building in Oklahoma City by Christian militants. The blast killed 168 people, including women and children, and injured over 680 people. The militants have been active ever since those dark days.

Jack Cody was born into a deeply religious family in Tulsa, Oklahoma. His father, who was a strict Baptist preacher, had put the fear of God in him at an early age. Jack believed he was predestined to wage war against the godless ones. He was seen by many as a messenger of God, he himself had no doubt about it. There was, driving him, a kind of rage, a deep psychological anger. Attacking the secularists was a means by which he could do the Lord's work in an active, meaningful way, and served as a conduit for his rage.

Jack Cody, a former Marine, had now become a guerrilla fighter, hiding out in secret campsites in the mountains with a small but growing band of followers. They started off by robbing several army surplus stores and gun shops in Boulder, Colorado. These robberies provided the supplies, weapons, and ammunition they would need to begin their guerilla movement.

One day, while Jack was reading the bible and praying, he received a call, which to him, was from a messenger of God. A theist sympathizer in the Army called him and told him about an arms shipment that would be heading to California from Missouri. The traitor had told him all the details he needed, including the date and time of the shipment, the exact route, and the types and numbers of weapons. The shipment would move through the Colorado Rockies on its way to California, and included XM8 assault rifles with grenade launchers and ammunition. For the theist guerillas it was a gift from God.

The army convoy had begun its trip two days earlier. The convoy consisted of a lead all-terrain vehicle with a driver, one-armed soldier in the front seat, and three armed soldiers in the back seat. Two large trucks followed the lead guard vehicle. Each truck had a driver and an armed soldier.

It had been an uneventful trip from Missouri through the seemingly endless plains of Kansas and into Colorado. The soldiers were enjoying the beautiful scenery of the Colorado Rocky Mountains. As they headed up a steep narrow winding canyon road, they came around a blind turn and saw a roadblock ahead. There was a flashing barricade and a sign labeled roadwork ahead. It was a construction crew working on the road. Not an unusual sight on the mountain roads of the west. There was an orange dump truck labeled with a Department of Transportation seal, and a yellow front loader working in the westbound lane. A flagman, standing in the westbound lane holding a stop/slow flagger paddle, was directing traffic. As the convoy approached the flagman he displayed the stop sign and approached the lead vehicle.

"Sorry for the delay fellows, it shouldn't be long," he said.

"No problem," replied the driver.

In an instant, the flagman pulled out an automatic rifle from underneath his vest and began shooting into the lead vehicle. Simultaneously, a van loaded with guerillas pulled up behind the rear truck. Eight armed guerillas jumped out of the van, split into two groups of four, and took up positions on both sides of the trucks. As the drivers and soldiers in the two trucks got out and attempted to return fire, they were cut down by the guerillas.

While a second flagman held traffic in the eastbound lane, the guerillas drove the dump truck and the front loader over to the disabled trucks. With the front loader they smashed in the rear door of the second truck and unloaded the crates of weapons and ammunition and placed them in the bucket of the front loader. From the front loader they moved the crates into the back of the dump truck. When they had finished loading the dump truck, the van with the guerillas picked up the flagman. They fled down the twisting canyon road in the van and dump truck, leaving the front loader, the convoy vehicles, and nine dead soldiers behind.

Back in Washington D.C., it was another busy day for President Adams. He had just completed a videoconference meeting with General Nathan Anderson, head of US Central Command (CENTCOM) and the Commander of US forces in Middle East, when the phone rang. It was the FBI Director, Stephen Weber.

"Mr. President, we just received word that heavily armed bandits attacked an army convoy in Colorado, killing nine soldiers, and escaping with one truckload of weapons and ammunition."

"Who was behind the attack?" asked the President.

"Based on preliminary information from the local authorities, it appears that a small time anti-government militia leader named Jack Cody led the convoy attack. He doesn't appear to be a significant threat."

"Well Mr. Weber, perhaps you should remember the Cuban communist, Fidel Castro. He started out as a two-bit thug and became the leader of a guerilla movement. After Castro attacked the army barracks in Santiago, the Batista regime arrested him, and planned to execute him, but instead spared his life. Six years later, after his revolution had overthrown the hated dictator Batista, he made his triumphant march into Havana and took power. We're not going to make the same mistake. He must be captured or killed immediately."

"Yes Sir, Mr. President."

The FBI director had gotten the message loud and clear and quickly escalated the case to a priority one.

The President had hardened over the years. After witnessing the senseless killing of thousands of innocent civilians he had learned the hard way that reason doesn't work on the unreasonable. He had also learned that you couldn't allow your adversaries any room to maneuver. Seemingly insignificant events could have an unexpected and sometimes enormous impact on the future.

President Adams had read about the guerilla wars of the past. The Spanish and Russian guerilla wars against Napoleon, Mao Tse-tung and the Chinese guerilla war against Japanese occupation and the American humiliation in the war against the Viet Cong guerillas in Viet Nam. He knew that guerilla movements usually started out with a small number of disgruntled individuals who formed small resistance groups with limited organization and weapons. As the groups gradually grew larger and acquired more weapons they would increase their attacks. They expanded their political operations as well, building support among the population through agitation, propaganda, and even buying support by providing money for health services, education, and food. As they grew to the size of a division they could mount serious attacks against the regular forces, eventually even defeating larger armies and countries. He had also learned that you fight guerillas with guerilla tactics. To win a guerilla war you cannot sit back and wait for the guerillas to attack. You have to be in constant attack mode, relentlessly pursuing and killing the guerilla leaders, before the movement has time to gain mass support.

A Visit to Dr. Edwards Lab

The United States had always counted on its technological superiority to win wars. Over the last century the annual military budget of the United States had been larger than the rest of the nations of the world combined. With a huge budget for research and development, the Department of Defense research labs were paradise to Dr. Edwards, whose true love was engineering, science and technology, not public policy and war. With war imminent, General Tillman paid a visit to Dr. Edwards's lab to see what kind of new technology he might have under development that could assist in the war effort. General Tillman entered the lab to find Dr. Edwards setting up a test of some new laser device.

"Looks like yet another laser device Dr. E," said the General.

"General Tillman, yes another laser device. But I think you're going to like this one."

"What does it do?"

"This is a laser based Raman spectroscopy device, otherwise known as the Raman Spectroscopy Explosive Residue Detection Unit (RSERDU). When a beam of light is impinged upon a sample, photons are absorbed by the material and scattered. The incident photon excites an electron into a higher virtual energy level and then decays back to a lower energy level, emitting a scattered photon. The energies of these transitions are plotted as spectrum. This spectrum can then be used to fingerprint substances. Using this new laser based system we can detect small amounts of residue from explosives and weapons on any kind of surface from a distance of up to 100 meters in real time. We no longer have to use those test strips that have to be in contact with the surface of the material."

"How does it work?"

"Explosives constantly give off particles and vapors. The particles transfer easily to solid surfaces. Detecting trace amounts of these particles indicates that the person or object has come in contact with the explosives at some point in time. This may also indicate the presence of large quantities of explosives, observe."

Dr Edwards placed a square piece of metal in a vice and walked back to his mounted laser device.

"Imagine that this piece of metal is a car door."

He activated the laser and there was a quick flash of light on the piece of metal. The screen on the laser device showed a spectrum and identified the substance as C4 plastic explosives residue.

As the General observed the read out on the screen he said, "Now that is amazing!"

"It's going to save many of our soldier's lives. They will now be able to detect explosives from a safe distance, and will be able to screen insurgents from a distance to determine if they are fighters or civilians, all in real-time."

"When can we have these deployed in the field?"

"We have finished the final prototype testing of our portable unit, and are moving into production and deployment next week."

"What else do you have for me?"

"We have a new version of the Ultra-wideband Radar Virtual Room (URVR) system which has been in production for about three months now. It is an ultra-wideband radar system that produces a three-dimensional picture of the space behind a wall from a distance of up to 100 meters. The pictures, which resemble those produced by color enhanced ultrasound, are detailed real-time, high-resolution pictures of the interior rooms of a building."

"Very nice," commented the General.

"And of course the old standby, the Automotive Disruption System (ADS), which uses high intensity radio waves, to disable automobiles and trucks by disrupting the electronics systems that allow the car to function. This system can disable a car from a distance of up to 100 meters. Then we have the Electronic Field Surveillance System (EFSS)."

The general looked at his watch. He knew he could be there all day listening to Dr. Edwards talk about his inventions and technology.

"Listen, Doc, those are all fantastic and I would like to see more but I really have to be going."

Startled and somewhat dismayed that the General didn't have more time to hear about all his devices he replied, "Oh, okay. Come back anytime, I am always working on many interesting projects."

"All right Doc. Thanks! I'll be in touch," the General replied as he left the lab.

Dr. Edwards had been very busy indeed. He was also involved in the development of high frequency ground penetrating radar for finding caves and tunnels. Ground penetrating radar uses electromagnetic wave propagation and scattering to image, locate and quantitatively identify changes in electrical and magnetic properties in the ground. The new satellite system could scan and map vast areas showing details down to one meter at depths of up to 1000 meters. With the new ground penetrating radar and the virtual room system, there was no place for the enemy to hide.

The Sacred Texts

While the battle was heating up in America, it was already hot in the Far East. Russian forces had already advanced deep into Kazakhstan, while Chinese forces moved into Nepal and Burma. They encountered very light resistance, and were making good progress on their drive toward the Islamic Front Nations, destroying every last vestige of religion as they raced towards the south.

The speed of the advance of the secularist forces surprised the theist leaders. An urgent meeting of the Council of Elders was called. The meeting was being held in Alexandria Egypt because of its prominence as a center for the antiquities trade. There was a conference on paleography being held in Alexandria, which was to be attended by the internationally recognized expert on antiquities, Professor Alexander Clark.

The Council had received news that the secularists were destroying bibles and copies of the Koran and the Torah in America. The Council members knew it was only a matter of time before the secularists would begin destroying all the sacred texts and that they would need help if they were to have any chance of saving the remaining copies. They needed someone they could trust, and someone who had access to the great libraries of the world if they were to be successful. That someone was Alexander Clark.

Professor Clark, also known as the Librarian, was a Professor of Philosophy at Oxford University and the Director of Scholarship and Collections at the British Library. Professor Clark was a world-renowned expert on ancient manuscripts and paleography. He was also a good Christian, and had the knowledge and the access to help save the sacred texts. The professor had been invited to the Council of Elders meeting to present the latest information on the sacred texts.

"As you know professor, the godless ones are on a crusade to destroy religion. In so doing, they wish to destroy the sacred texts. We have called upon your services to help us secure the sacred texts before they can be destroyed," explained Nicholas.

"The secularists know that to completely destroy religion, they must destroy the sacred texts. The sacred texts are the foundation of our faith, without them we have nothing," replied Professor Clark.

"What can you tell us about the sacred texts?" asked Elijah.

The professor began his presentation, "As you know, there is still disagreement between various Christian sects about which books belong to the Bible. There are books included in the Septuagint and Vulgate, which are excluded from the Jewish and Protestant canons of the Old Testament. Both the western Catholic and eastern Orthodox churches base their Old Testaments on the Septuagint, a Greek translation of the Hebrew Old Testament."

"The oldest existing version of the New Testament, long preserved at St. Catherine's monastery on Mount Sinai, is now in the British Library. The British Library's New Testament is pocket-sized, bound in crimson leather, and richly illustrated. There is also the Stuttgart Copy, which is complete with title page and preserved in its original binding, it resides in the Württemberg State Library in Stuttgart. The only other known copy of Tyndale's New Testament, in St. Paul's Cathedral, London, has 59 leaves missing. Tyndale's Worms New Testament, which was translated from the Greek original, was the first copy of the New Testament printed in English. In the spring of 1994 the British Library acquired this New Testament for a little over £1,000,000."

"Apart from the two copies of the Gutenberg Bible in the British Library there are 46 other complete copies of the Bible or substantial fragments worldwide. Six of these are in the United Kingdom. The Bodleian Library in Oxford has a complete copy printed on paper. There is a copy in Cambridge University Library and Eton College has a copy on paper. At Lambeth Palace in London, the palace of the Archbishop of Canterbury, there is a copy of Volume 2, printed on vellum. The John Rylands Library in Manchester has a copy on paper, and there is a copy in the National Library of Scotland."

"The oldest surviving copies of the Koran were discovered in the ancient Great Mosque of Sa'na in 1972, when the building was being restored after heavy rainfall. Until this discovery there were three ancient copies of the Koran. One copy in the Library of Tashkent in Uzbekistan, and another in the Topkapi Museum in Istanbul, Turkey, date from the eighth century. A copy preserved in the British Library in London, known as the Ma'il manuscript, dates from the late seventh century."

"The Dead Sea scrolls were discovered between 1947 and 1960 at sites along the Dead Sea. The scrolls date to 150 BC and 5 BC. In addition to the oldest known versions of some Old Testament books, the scrolls include long-lost originals of several books of the Apocrypha and non-biblical Jewish religious works such as the books of Enoch, Jubilees, and the Testaments of the Twelve Patriarchs. Most of the originals of the scrolls are at the Rockefeller Museum in East Jerusalem, the rest are at the Israel Museum's Shrine of the Book in Jerusalem. Fragments of the Dead Sea scrolls are also on display at the Archeological Museum in Amman, Jordan."

"There are three main versions of the Hebrew Bible. There is the Masoretic text of the Torah of which the oldest known copy is the Aleppo Codex. The scribe Shlomo Ben-Buya'a copied the Codex over one thousand years ago. In 1958, the Aleppo Codex was brought to Jerusalem, where it remains in the Shrine of the Book at the Israel Museum. The oldest complete text is the Leningrad Codex, which dates to the tenth century AD. Then there is the Septuagint, which is a Greek translation of the Torah, made under Ptolemy in the third century BC and the Peshitta, a translation of the Christian Bible into Syriac, a variant of Aramaic. The earliest known copy of the Peshitta dates to 445-460 AD. The Leningrad Codex is in St. Petersburg, Russia, at the Russian National Library where it has been since the mid-1800s."

"The Vedas are the most important sacred texts of Hinduism. The most important of the Vedas is the Rig Veda, which is a collection of 1,028 Hymns written in praise of the most important gods of the Vedic period. The Upanishads are a collection of writings composed between 600 - 200 BC. They are concerned with learning about Brahman, the all-pervading life force, and the relationship between Brahman and the universe. The British Library collection of Hindu texts and associated literature has been built up continuously since the end of the eighteenth century when European scholars first began a serious study of Hinduism. Acquired in 1789, the collection includes the earliest manuscript set of the Vedas to reach Europe."

Professor Clark was finishing his presentation when there was a knock on the door. It was a messenger with a note for the Archbishop. The Archbishop read the note and with a look of dismay said, "The Russians have just invaded Kazakhstan and are moving rapidly to the south."

"Nicholas, we must move quickly if we are to get to the Library of Tashkent in Uzbekistan before the Russians do. There are other mosques with valuables that must be moved and we have no forces or defenses in the north," pleaded Mustafa.

"There is no way we will be able to secure all of the sacred texts, we must focus on getting the most complete copies for each of the major religions," said Surya.

"We must act quickly and get to the sacred texts before the secularists, or they will all be destroyed. I will secure the Codex Sinaiticus New Testament, the Tyndale's New Testament, the Rig Veda, and the Ma'il Koran from the British Library. My associate Dmitry Ivanov at St. Petersburg State University will secure the Leningrad Codex from the Russian National Library. The texts will be shipped to Khartoum, Sudan and stored there until the preparation of the final storage site is complete," said Professor Clark.

"We wish you Godspeed on your mission professor. Please let us know if you need any assistance. We will meet again soon. I will contact you with the time and location," said Nicholas.

With the news of the rapid advance of secularist forces, the meeting ended so the theists could work on securing the sacred texts. Professor Clark returned to London and immediately began his work while the others returned to the fight.

The Librarian's Mission

Upon his return to London from the Alexandria Council meeting, Professor Clark began working on his plan and preparations to save the sacred texts. Fortunately, he already had most of the things he needed. He had special cases for the sacred texts, and there were plenty of readily available forgeries and replicas of the sacred documents. Many art and manuscript forgeries are so well done that even experts have a difficult time determining their authenticity. His plan was simple. Go to the library with the replicas in his briefcase, replace the original texts with the replicas, put the originals in his briefcase and exit the library.

With the preparations complete the day to retrieve the sacred texts had arrived. Professor Clark was feeling extremely anxious. He had never done anything unethical or illegal in his entire life. He tried to calm down and concentrate on the importance of his mission. He thought about William Tyndale who sacrificed everything for his beliefs. It was William Tyndale's translation and publication of the New Testament that opened the bible to the masses. For his reformist views and challenges to the church and state he paid with his life. Charged with treason and heresy, he was strangled and burnt at the stake.

Now it was the professor's turn and there was no turning back. The professor traveled to the British Library to retrieve the sacred texts. He arrived at the front entrance and entered the building.

He walked up to the security station where he was greeted by the security guard.

"Good evening Professor Clark, more ancient texts?" asked the security guard.

"Yes, more ancient texts," replied the professor.

As the Director of Scholarship and Collections at the library and having spent countless hours at the library studying and analyzing ancient texts, Professor Clark was a familiar figure at the library. He signed in and took the stairs up to the rare books section of the library.

With full access to all areas of the library he quickly went from case to case replacing the original sacred texts with the replicas. With the substitutions complete he carefully wrapped the sacred texts in protective cloth, placed them in his briefcase, and headed back down to the ground floor. With his heart racing he stopped at the security station to sign out.

"Short night tonight," said the security guard.

"Yes, just checking in some new material," replied the professor.

"Good evening," said the guard.

"Good evening to you," said the professor.

Once he had made his way through the security station the professor breathed a sigh of relief and his heart rate decreased. As he was just about to reach the exit, suddenly he heard the guard calling his name. His heart rate shot back up.

"Professor Clark!" yelled the security guard.

The professor froze and slowly turned around. The guard approached him.

"I am glad I caught you Professor Clark," said the security guard.

The professor thought his actions had been discovered and he had failed his mission.

"You left your ID card at the security station," said the security guard.

In his stressed condition he didn't remember placing his identification card on the top of the security station. The professor regained his composure and replied, "Thank you, I don't even remember putting it down."

"Quite all right professor, see you again soon," said the security guard.

"Yes, see you again soon," said the professor.

Feeling better but still traumatized from the whole ordeal, he turned and headed for the exit.

Back in his apartment, he removed the sacred texts from his briefcase and began placing them in specially designed cases that would preserve the texts for centuries to come. To protect the sacred texts from ultra-violet rays, oxygen, and fluctuations in humidity they were placed in hermetically sealed aluminum cases that were covered with two layers of special glass. The air inside the cases was replaced with helium, an inert gas that doesn't interact with parchment.

After the texts had been carefully sealed in their cases they were crated and shipped to Khartoum, Sudan, in Northern Africa. From Khartoum they were transported by truck to Nairobi, Kenya. The Librarian had been working with a local Christian missionary group to build a vault deep in the Aberdare range to store the sacred texts.

The misty and rainy forests in the Aberdare range had served the Mau-Mau guerillas well during their insurgency against the British colonial administration. Located in the Central Highlands west of Mount Kenya the area is home to lush vegetation, mountain streams and spectacular waterfalls. The landscape is dominated by foggy rain forest. At elevations above 2000 meters the rain forest gives way to bamboo jungles. With many remote and inaccessible areas, the Kenyan jungle was a perfect place to hide the sacred texts.

It was a long, exhausting, and dangerous trip from Khartoum to Nairobi by truck and an even more arduous hike into the Aberdare range to the jungle vault. It would have been a difficult trip for a young man, but for a man approaching 80 years old it was an amazing journey of determination.

Despite the exhaustion and the hardships, the professor had completed his mission. The sacred texts had been safely secured in their jungle vault. He knew it was just a matter of time before he would be discovered as the person responsible for removing the sacred texts so he returned to London to gather his belongings and move to Alexandria, Egypt. At least there, he hoped, he could continue his studies.

In the event that the Librarian or the Council members were captured or killed, the Librarian had hidden an encrypted map showing the location of the sacred texts in an obscure book at the British Library. He believed that one day, the vault would be opened, and the sacred texts could be returned to the faithful.

The Captain and the Car

Ashley Morgan, a nurse at Halifax Medical Center in Daytona Beach, Florida, had just finished another shift, and was preparing to go home when Dr. Williams met her in the hall.

"Hello Ashley, how's it going today?" asked Dr. Williams.

"Actually, it was a pretty good day, but I'm beat. I need a vacation."

"I know the feeling. Say, speaking of vacations, I have been looking for someone who might be interested in driving a car out to Tyndall Air Force Base. My son is stationed there, and has not been able to get away to get his new car."

Dr. Williams was more interested in playing matchmaker than getting his sons car out of the garage. He had always liked Ashley, she was very bright and hard working, and she sincerely cared about the patients in her care. His son Kyle was too busy flying airplanes to find a wife and settle down. He thought that if Kyle could meet Ashley it might help him along.

Dr. Williams' son was Capt. Kyle "Cowboy" Williams. He was given the nickname "Cowboy" because he was originally from Whitefish, Montana, and everybody always thought that if you were from Montana, you must be a cowboy. He graduated from the Air Force Academy with a degree in aeronautical engineering, completed his flight training, and had achieved his boyhood dream of becoming a fighter pilot, flying the modernized version of the Lockheed Joint Strike Fighter the F-35EX Lightning.

Ashley had seen a picture of Dr. Williams's son in his office and had always thought he was a very handsome young man. Since she was single and really didn't have anything else to do, it sounded like it could be fun.

"I could use a few days off. I've been meaning to get over to Panama City and Destin for some time now, but I just haven't gotten around to it. Let me check my schedule and I'll get back to you."

"Just let me know when you can go, and I will make the arrangements."

It appeared that the good doctor's matchmaking plans were off to a good start.

Ashley headed home, poured herself a glass of Merlot, and sat down at her computer to get the directions and drive time to Panama City. It was a straight shot across the state on Interstate Highway 10, and would only take about six hours. Since it was a fairly short drive, and Dr. Williams was going to pay for everything, she decided to make the trip. The next day, she called Dr. Williams to make the arrangements, and the following weekend she was off for Panama City.

Capt. Williams had just returned from a flight-planning meeting for a training exercise when he heard a knock at the door. He opened the door and to his surprise, found a woman standing on the front porch. The woman had long curly blonde hair, and she was wearing sunglasses. She looked and dressed like a fashion model or a Hollywood movie star. Capt. Williams had never seen her before so he figured she must have the wrong house.

"Are you Kyle Williams?" she asked.

"Yes, ma'am, I'm Capt. Williams," he replied.

"I have a car for you."

"A car," he said in a perplexed tone.

"My name is Ashley Morgan. I work with your father at Halifax Medical Center. Your father asked me if I would deliver your car to you. I didn't have anything else to do, so here I am."

"Wow! That's tremendous! I've wanted to get back home and get my car but I just haven't had time."

"Well you have it now," she said as she handed him the keys.

"You must be tired after your trip, please come in."

"Not really. It was all interstate highways so the drive wasn't too bad," she replied.

Ashley entered the Spartan home. As she scanned the interior of the house, she thought to herself that Capt. William must be a minimalist. There was only a couch, a coffee table, and a television in the front room. Looking down the hall into the kitchen she could see that the only furniture in the kitchen was an old card table with two folding chairs. It was a good thing she didn't bring any of her friends; they would have had a hard time finding a chair.

"How long have you known my father?" he asked.

"About four years now."

"I'm going to have to speak to him about not telling me about you."

"He's a very busy man, and works incredibly hard."

"I know. I keep trying to get him to slow down, but he refuses. Would you like something to drink?"

"A Diet Coke would be nice."

He walked into the kitchen and grabbed a Diet Coke out of the refrigerator. As he walked back into the front room he asked, "Where are you staying?"

"I was going to get a room over at the Edgewater Beach Resort."

"I'd hate for you to have to stay in a hotel. You could stay here. I can sleep on the couch."

"I don't want to be a burden."

"It's the least I can do to repay you for driving my car over. Let me get you things out of the car."

"Well, if you're sure I'm not going to be in the way. May I use your bathroom to freshen up?"

"Sure, it's right down the hall on the left. I'll get your bags."

Kyle was so excited with the prospect of spending time with Ashley that he tripped and fell running up the front porch stairs with her bags. He managed to stumble back to the bedroom with her bags when Ashley emerged from the bathroom. Kyle showed her the bedroom and gave her the nickel tour of the rest of the house. After he completed the tour he asked her if she would like to go out and get a pizza. Ashley loved pizza, and after her trip she was starving, so she thought that would be marvelous.

They arrived at the pizza parlor and walked up to the counter to place their order.

"I'll have a large pizza with extra cheese, sausage, and black olives," he said.

"Will that be all?" asked the server.

"Oh, I'm sorry, what would you like Ashley?"

With a look of surprise Ashley responded, "I'll have the same only with green peppers and mushrooms."

She had thought Kyle was ordering for both of them. She couldn't believe he had ordered before her. Kyle seemed to be such a gentleman with impeccable manners. She wasn't sure if he was just teasing her, or if he was just too hungry to think straight.

Seemingly unaware of his error, Kyle gave her a strange look, and thought that she must be mighty hungry to be able to put away a large pizza. As they ate their pizzas they talked about their families, the different places they had been in Florida, and the vacations they would like to take someday. They finished their pizzas, left the pizza parlor and decided to go for a short walk along the beach. The incident at the pizza parlor was soon forgotten, and they were laughing and joking as they walked. Ashley was feeling very comfortable being around Kyle, and would occasionally bump into him as they walked. He was like a rock. She could tell he must be in incredible shape. She knew that pilots had to be in great shape both mentally and physically to be able to fly high performance aircraft.

They finally arrived back at the house, and were getting ready to shutdown for the night when Kyle asked, "Would you like to go on a picnic tomorrow? There's a great place up on the bay called Eden Gardens."

"That would be very nice."

Ashley was exhausted from the drive, and all the activities of the day, and said goodnight as she entered the bedroom. Kyle dutifully took his position on the couch.

The next day as they were leaving the base for their picnic, they ran into Kyle's best friend Henry Gonzalez, and his fiancée Anna Perez.

"Henry, what's up?" said Kyle.

"Not much to it. Headin to the beach for some R&R," replied Henry.

"Hi Anna, how are you?" Kyle continued.

"I'm doing fine, thanks. Who's this?" Anna had never seen Kyle with a girl like Ashley before. She had tried to set him up with girls before but none of them ever worked out. So she was curious to find out who this pretty new girl was.

"Oh, I'm sorry, this is Ashley Morgan. She drove my car down from Daytona Beach. "She's a nurse at Halifax Medical Center where my dad works. Ashley, this is my best friend, and the best Crew Chief in the United States Air Force, Henry Gonzalez and his fiancée Anna Perez."

Anna extended her hand and said, "Very nice to meet you."

"It's a pleasure to meet you," replied Ashley.

"Where are you guys off to?" asked Henry.

"We're heading up to Eden Gardens for a picnic," replied Kyle.

"That sounds great. The grounds and the old house are beautiful," said Anna.

"Well, we had better get going. You guys have fun at the beach."

"It was a pleasure to meet you," said Ashley.

They said their goodbyes and were off on their excursion to Eden Gardens. Eden Gardens State Park was home to the historic Wesley Homestead, which is surrounded by majestic moss draped oaks. Kyle had always loved Spanish moss, with its silvery-gray threadlike mass, hanging from the trees in the south. The main attractions at the park are the ornamental gardens, and an abundance of camellias and azaleas with their beautiful spring flowers. They found a great picnic site overlooking Choctawhatchee Bay. It was a beautiful warm sunny day, with a gentle breeze coming off the bay, the turquoise water glowing in the afternoon sun, the palm trees gently swaying in the breeze.

"Why did you decide to become a fighter pilot?" asked Ashley.

"When I was a kid, my father took me to Elgin Air Force Base to watch the Thunderbirds precision flying team. I was in total amazement at the skill of the pilots and the speed and agility of the aircraft. That was all it took. I decided right then and there, that I was going to be flying one of those planes some day."

"What did your father think about you wanting to become a fighter pilot?"

"I think he really wanted me to follow in his footsteps and become a doctor, even though he never came right out and told me that I should become a doctor. But if he was disappointed, he never showed it. He is a firm believer that independent thought produces the best outcomes. What about you? What does your father do?"

"He's a doctor too. And, he does want me to become a doctor."

"Are you going to become a doctor?"

"I've given it a lot of thought. I just don't know if I have what it takes mentally and physically to do it."

"You seem to be very smart, and you look like you're in great shape to me. I'm sure you could do it if you really wanted to."

"You're very kind. Ashley got uncomfortable talking about going to medical school, she had lamented over it for months, so she quickly changed the subject.

"How long have you known Henry?"

"Believe it or not, Henry and I go back to the fifth grade. We went to high school together, played football together, went on our first date together, joined the Air Force together, well we've done just about everything together. He's like a brother to me. You couldn't ask for a better friend, or a better human being than Henry."

"It's nice to have good friends. It's a rarity to have friends that go back to elementary school."

They finished their picnic lunch and Kyle said, "I know this really great place to watch the sunset. Would you like to go?"

"Sure, that would be great."

They packed up the picnic basket and headed to the beach. There was a little place down on Gulf Drive called Schooners where they count down to the precise moment the sun dips below the horizon, and then they fire an old cannon.

The weekend went quickly and the time had come for Ashley to head back to Daytona Beach. They arrived at the airport terminal. Kyle got of the car, opened the door for Ashley, and pulled her bags out of the trunk.

"Thank you so much Kyle. I had a really nice time."

"I did too. I'd love to be able to see you again."

"I would like that too."

Ashley gave him a hug, kissed him on the cheek and said, "Call me next time you get a weekend pass."

As Ashley turned and walked inside the terminal, Kyle just stood and watched her walk away. He felt a sinking feeling in his stomach. He was sad to see her go. Even though he had only been with her for a short time, he felt like a lovesick puppy. When he was with Ashley, it was like the rest of the world with all its flaws and problems didn't exist. Spending time with her was the one of the most enjoyable experiences he had had in a long time. He had never met a girl like Ashley before, and he knew he would miss her very much.

On the flight back all Ashley could think about was Kyle, and what he had told her about going to medical school. She had a great time in Panama City and really liked Kyle. He was a real gentleman, always polite and courteous, and he had a certain confidence and discipline about him. He had an easy natural smile that made you feel good, plus he was smart, energetic, and fun. She couldn't wait to see him again.

Ashley arrived home late Sunday afternoon from the airport. The taxi dropped her of in front of her house. As she walked up the front sidewalk she saw something on the front porch. She walked up onto the front porch, and there leaning against the front door was a beautiful bouquet of long stem red roses with a note. She opened the note. It was from Kyle.

Ashley,

Thanks again for a wonderful weekend. You sure are fun! Even though you just left, I miss you already. I can't wait to see you again. Take care.

Kyle

The roses clinched the deal. Ashley had been thinking that she really liked Kyle. Now she knew for sure. She couldn't wait to see him again.

Discovery at the British Library

The British government had started its confiscation of religious materials when it was discovered that the collection of rare bibles, and Islamic and Hindu texts held in the British Library were forgeries. They had also discovered that it was Professor Clark who had been the one responsible for the replacement of the originals with fraudulent copies. Their discovery came too late. Professor Clark had already transported the originals out of the country, and was preparing to leave the country as well. The British authorities immediately put out a communication for Professor Clark's arrest.

Attempting to stay one step ahead of the authorities, Professor Clark had finished packing his belongings and getting his affairs in order. He left London's Heathrow Airport on a flight to Athens, Greece. As he was transferring to the flight to Egypt, two men in suits and two police officers approached him.

"Professor Clark?" asked one of the men.

"Yes, I am Professor Clark."

"Professor Clark, we have a warrant for your arrest."

"I have done nothing wrong. I am a professor at Oxford."

"Yes professor, we know. We also know that you have stolen several books from the British Library and replaced them with forgeries. You will have to come with us."

One of the police officers grabbed the professor by the arm, and they escorted him to the airport's security office. Once in the office they sat him down and began questioning him. One of the men wearing a suit began the questioning.

"Now professor why don't you tell us what you have done with the books?"

"I'm sorry; I cannot provide you with that information."

"Why are you working for the theists?"

"I am not working for the theists."

"We have information that you met with the theist leaders in Egypt last month. Is that true?"

"I have nothing further to say."

"Well then professor, I am afraid that we have no choice. Due to your role in the theft of the books, and your involvement with the theists, we consider you to be an enemy combatant. You will be charged with aiding and abetting a terrorist organization and will be transferred immediately to the prison at Guantanamo Bay. You have one last chance to tell us what you have done with the books."

"I'm afraid I can't do that."

"I'm confident some time in solitary confinement will help you change your mind."

"But I am a British citizen, what about my rights?"

"You have chosen to take sides with the terrorists. Terrorists have no rights. Enjoy your trip to Cuba professor."

The men in the suits left the office. The police officers placed the professor in a holding cell while arrangements were made to transport him to Cuba.

Guantanamo Bay has served as holding facility for suspected terrorists and enemy combatants since the war against the Taliban and al Qaeda in Afghanistan following the September 11th 2001 attacks against the United States. Supporters of the use of Guantanamo Bay to secure terrorists believed that certain protections of the Geneva Convention did not apply to al-Qaeda or Taliban fighters. They believe that Article III of the Geneva Convention only applies to uniformed soldiers and guerrillas who wear distinctive insignia, bear arms openly, and abide by the rules of war, and that terrorists, who are not recognized as soldiers, don't deserve to be treated as soldiers.

Guantanamo Bay Naval Base is located on 45 square miles of land and water at the southeastern end of Cuba. The United States leased the area for use as a fueling station and naval base following the Cuban-American Treaty of 1903. The base also provides protection for US Navy and Coast Guard operations in the Caribbean.

The Council of Elders was meeting in Tripoli, Libya, when they received word about the capture of the Librarian by secularist forces. The Archbishop broke the news, "We have received news that the Librarian has been captured by the secularist authorities in Athens, Greece, as he was attempting to flee to Alexandria, Egypt. Fortunately, he was able to secure the sacred texts before his capture. God willing, the sacred texts will now survive the scorched earth campaign of the godless heathens."

"Isn't there anything we can do to help the Librarian?" asked Surya.

"Unfortunately, there is little we can do for him now except fight for the principles and ideals contained in the sacred texts. Because of his dedication and courage, the foundations of our faith will survive. There are more urgent matters that need to be addressed."

"Mustafa, I understand you have been working on the planning for a series of attacks against the infidels," said Nicholas.

"Yes Nicholas. We have planned five simultaneous attacks on military and civilian targets."

"I thought we agreed that we were not going to target civilians," said Surya.

"We have to use terror as a weapon. We have no choice," responded Mustafa.

"As long as I am Chairman of this Council, there will be no targeting of civilians. If we start killing women and children we will loose the support of the people we are fighting for," said an angry Nicholas.

"It is too late. The process is already in motion. The cells have their orders, we dare not contact them," explained Mustafa.

"No more civilians will be targeted, is that understood?" demanded Nicholas.

Mustafa was ruthless and a firm believer that the end justifies the means. If killing civilians furthered the cause they were just a causality of war. Reluctantly, and with an obvious lack of sincerity Mustafa agreed.

"No more civilians, only military targets," he said as he continued outlining the attacks, "The attacks are planned for next week and will take place in Spain, Turkey, Turkmenistan, Afghanistan, and Pakistan. Allah willing, we expect to inflict heavy causalities on the crusaders from our sacred bombers."

The news about the planned attacks on civilians increased the existing tensions within the members of the council. There were ongoing disagreements over strategy and tactics, and the distrust that existed between the former enemies continued to escalate.

The Commander and the Librarian

Captain Thomas Baker, the Commander of Guantanamo Bay Naval Base, stood and observed as the new prisoners were brought into the processing center. As the prisoners marched forward for inspection the Librarian stumbled and fell out of line. One of the guards swung around and gave him an elbow strike to the back of the head knocking him to the ground. The Librarian was on his knees when the guard noticed he was wearing a gold chain with a locket shaped like a cross. The guard grabbed the chain and ripped it from the Librarian's neck.

"Contraband is not allowed, now get back into line!" commanded the guard.

Capt. Baker walked quickly toward the guard. "Don't you know who this prisoner is?" the captain asked the guard.

The guard snapped to attention and replied, "Yes Sir, this is prisoner number 2718, Sir."

As the aggravated commander grabbed the necklace from the guard he shouted "You idiot! This is the Librarian, keeper of the sacred texts. He will not be harmed. Is that clear?"

"Yes Sir!" replied the cowering guard.

The Captain turned to the Librarian and said, "My apologies for the rough treatment Professor Clark, it will not happen again."

"May I please have my cross back, it is very important to me?" asked the Librarian.

"I'm sorry Professor; the possession of jewelry by prisoners is prohibited."

The Commander finished his inspection of the prisoners and returned to his office. The Commander's office was very organized. On his desk there was only a flat screen computer display and a telephone. The furnishings were modest with only a conference table and chairs, and some old filing cabinets. On one wall there is a large map of the world. On the other side of the office there were wall-to-wall built in bookshelves totally filled with books. The Commander loved books and was an avid reader. He had an endless thirst for knowledge, and would read any time he got a free moment.

The prison conditions at Guantanamo Bay were not comfortable, but they were much better than the majority of the prisons where suspected theist sympathizers were being held. Most of the prisoners were living in better conditions than they did before they were captured. The cells for most of the prisoners had wire mesh walls, with a corrugated metal roof, sitting on a concrete base. Each prisoner was given a foam sleeping mat, one blanket, two buckets, and a one-quart canteen. The high profile prisoners, like the Librarian, were kept in solitary confinement inside one of the interrogation buildings.

The following day, Capt. Baker was reviewing the Librarian's file when there was a knock on his office door.

"Enter! The door is unlocked," said the Commander.

The door opened, it was a guard with the Librarian.

"Professor Clark, please come in and have a seat. Would you care for something to drink, some tea perhaps?"

"No thank you," answered the Librarian.

The Commander returned to his desk and sat down.

"I was just reviewing your file. Tell me professor, exactly how were you captured?"

"I was attempting to travel from London to Egypt when I was arrested in Greece while transferring to another plane."

"What was your final destination in Egypt?"

"I was on my way to Alexandria."

"What was the purpose of your trip?"

"There was to be a meeting of scholars to discuss the preservation of archeological sites and artifacts."

"Did the artifacts include any of the sacred texts?"

"There was a concern that some of the remaining sacred texts and artifacts would be destroyed."

"I don't suppose you would want to tell me where the sacred texts are being hidden?"

"I cannot provide you with that information."

"I understand. We will have plenty of time to discuss the sacred texts."

"Why am I being held? I am merely a university professor," asked the Librarian.

"As of now, you are considered a terrorist sympathizer and an enemy combatant. Very serious charges," replied the Commander.

"But I am not a terrorist. I have never supported terrorism."

"Perhaps not, but you have been linked to the theist leadership."

"When will I be released?"

"That all depends on your cooperation. If you cooperate, your incarceration could be a short period of time; otherwise you will probably be here for a very long time."

As Capt. Baker continued reviewing the Librarian's file he remarked, "I see from your file that you have a Masters degree in history from the University of Oxford."

"Why yes, that's correct."

"I too have a Masters degree in History. Since you are going to be with us for a very long time, I look forward to many discussions about history and the current state of affairs."

"I am pleased that you chose history as a field of study, but I do not plan on being here for an extended period of time."

"That is all for now professor. We will talk again soon."

The commander called the guard in to take the Librarian back to his cell.

The Battle for Turkey

Turkey, with its strategic location between Europe and the Muslim world, had become a focal point in the war. The center of U.S. operations in Turkey is Incirlik Air Base. Incirlik has a long history of support for U.S. military operations in the region and has served as a hub for U.S. support for Turkey during natural disaster assistance and humanitarian emergencies.

The base was the main U-2 operating location until May 1960, when Francis Gary Powers' U-2 aircraft was shot down by Soviet surface-to-air missiles over Sverdlovsk. In response to the 9/11 terrorist attacks on the World Trade Center towers in New York, the base severed as a major hub in support of Operation Enduring Freedom. Thousands of soldiers have passed through Incirlik as their first stop on the way back from the field of battle to the United States.

Turkey has a history of implementing radical change for the good of the state. National hero Mustafa Kemal, who was later honored with the title Ataturk, "Father of the Turks," founded modern Turkey in 1923 from the Turkish remnants of the defeated Ottoman Empire. The Ottoman Empire was a Muslim empire, based in Constantinople, now Istanbul, which controlled southeastern Europe, the Middle East, and most of North Africa between the sixteenth and eighteenth centuries. The Ottoman Empire came to an end after World War I when it became The Republic of Turkey. Turkey joined the United

Nations in 1945 and in 1952 became a member of the North Atlantic Treaty Organization (NATO).

For Ataturk, modernization meant Westernization. He initiated a series of radical economic, political, and social reforms, which he considered of vital importance for the salvation and survival of his people. These reforms included suppressing religious orders, closing religious schools, secularizing the public education system, abolishing the fez, giving women equal political footing with men, changing the alphabet from Arabic to Latin letters and eliminating Arab words in the Turkish language, instituting a tradition of last names, creating a secular republican form of government, and abolishing the caliphate and Islamic law, which established a secular state by ending any connection between the state and religion.

For Turkey's leaders, the decision to follow the UN and EU declarations on religion was a matter of survival. Like Ataturk before them, the Turkish leaders believed that radical actions, including the elimination of the remaining religious groups, and the closing of mosques and Orthodox churches were necessary for the survival of the nation.

The radical actions of the government were swift and harsh and resulted in the mass exodus of 2074. The scale of the migration of people from Turkey to the Islamic Front states was the greatest migration of people since 12 million people became refuges as Muslims in India fled to Pakistan, and Hindus fled to India as a result of the British partition of India in 1947.

Some of the emigrants had vehicles, some were on horseback, but the majority traveled on foot. The mass wave of people moved like a thick syrup in an endless river. The long exodus was a constant struggle for survival. As resources dwindled, violence between the fleeing masses escalated. Men, women, and children were commonly beaten with clubs and stones and left to die. The stench of death hung in the air as the numbers of dead increased. Their agony only intensified by the extreme temperatures and the swarming insects. It was a wretched journey, with the thirst and hunger, the fatigue, and the endless miles. Many started throwing things away until, at the end of their journey, they had almost nothing left. Tens of thousands died during the migration. The lucky few that survived faced an uncertain future in a hostile land.

Although many of the faithful had fled, pockets of resistance formed to fight against the Turkish government reforms. Eventually, the rebel army became more organized and grew large enough to begin fighting a guerilla war against coalition forces. The largest of the rebel armies formed in the provinces of Rize and Trabzon and set up camps high in the rugged Kackar Mountains in the Northern Anatolian range. From these mountain camps, the insurgents would strike when coalition forces were least expecting it, and then vanish into the forbidding mountains.

Trabzon city, the provincial capital of Trabzon province, is a gritty industrial town situated on a table like promontory above the harbor on the coast of the Black Sea. Home to the Sumela Monastery and other Byzantine relics, it lies astride the road from Istanbul to Iran and was an important meeting point for international trade. Trabzon has strategic importance because of its location at the beginning of the road that connects the Black Sea coast to Iran and its close proximity to the Zigana Pass. The two kilometer long Zigana Tunnel now circumvents the ancient inhospitable Zigana Pass, which led to the Armenian frontier.

The province of Rize, located on the eastern coast of the Black Sea and just east of Trabzon, is green and lush all year round and surrounded by mountains with chestnut and beech tree forests. Tea plantations and citrus orchards cover the terraced landscape with the bright green tea bushes covering entire mountainsides. On the coast, where there are many tea-processing plants, you can smell the tea in the air.

Army Rangers were the first American forces to move into Northern Turkey. The Rangers were patrolling and attacking insurgents in the provinces of Trabzon, and Rize. The Turkish armed forces had already taken control of most of the country with the exception of the border areas of Armenia, Georgia, Iran, and Syria.

Desperate Measures

As the children settled into their seats their teacher, Maria Milionis, brought the class to order. Maria was a strict instructor but she was a dedicated teacher and cared greatly for the children. As a child she had learned from her father the importance of self-discipline and self-reliance in leading a happy and successful life. Even though she could be strict, her pretty smile and cheerful personality made her one of the children's favorite teachers.

Although Maria was a very beautiful woman with a well-shaped figure, she had always tried to dress modestly and hide her beauty. She preferred to be judged on her knowledge and performance rather than on her looks, and in a dangerous world it was best not to draw attention to oneself.

While classes continued inside the school, outside a Ranger patrol had started moving down the street toward the school. Ranger patrols were never routine. One day they could be handing out candy to children, the next day they could be engaged in a firefight, fighting for their life. This day, the patrol started off quiet enough. The Ranger team had received intelligence that insurgents were planning attacks in the Trabzon area. Their mission was to perform a sweep of the area and capture or kill any insurgents they could find.

The patrols in the city were always carried out in a slow and methodical pattern. In an urban setting, the enemy could be hiding in doorways and alleyways, there could be snipers on the rooftops, and they could be disguised as non-combatants concealing both their identity and their weapons. Urban reconnaissance was always a dangerous business.

Captain Jake Collins was the team leader for the Army Rangers in Trabzon. Capt. Collins, otherwise known as 'The Machine' for his incredible strength and endurance, graduated from West Point Military Academy with degrees in physics and Middle Eastern studies. He had a 3rd degree black belt in Tae Kwon Do, and before entering West Point, was the Texas State Tae Kwon Do Champion. He was tough as shoe leather, but was passionate about the welfare of the men in his squad.

The Army Rangers are elite soldiers of the United States Special Forces. The Ranger program is the Army's most rigorous leadership training school. Of the 3,300 soldiers who begin the grueling nine-week course each year, fewer than half finish. Half of those, who eventually go on to graduate, had to repeat one of the course's four segments before they could wear the coveted Ranger Tab.

His training had made him mentally and physically tough. After making it through West Point and Ranger school, he believed that there wasn't anything he couldn't accomplish. It gave him the ability to persevere no matter how long something took, or how much pain was involved. Mental and physical fitness are mutually dependent. He knew you couldn't be physically tough if you were not mentally tough. The mission was always everyone's first concern, but as an officer his first priority was to ensure the welfare of the men assigned to him. His comfort and preferences always came last.

As the Ranger patrol moved down the street, Capt. Collins, observed a man walking into a school with what looked like a small backpack. At first he didn't think much about it. Suddenly, the man ran out of the school and started running down the street. Capt. Collins noticed that he no longer had the backpack and knew that something was wrong. He had seen backpack bombs used before, but he had a hard time believing that someone would blow up a school full of children.

Since there seemed to be no other explanation for the man leaving the school in such a hurry Capt. Collins radioed the rest of his team and ordered them to go after the fleeing man while he investigated the school. If it was a trap and the backpack contained a bomb he didn't want to lose his whole team. Capt. Collins ran to the front door and entered the school. Inside the front door was an entrance hall. On the right side of the entrance hall there was a door labeled gymnasium. On the left side there was a girl's restroom and boy's restroom. Straight ahead was another hallway that appeared to lead to the classrooms.

He quickly looked around the hallway for the backpack. It was nowhere to be found. Next, he entered the gymnasium to see if there were any students or any sign of the backpack, still no sign of the backpack or any students. He knew that if the backpack contained a bomb he would have to act fast. He ran back out of the gymnasium and headed down the hallway that led to the classrooms. As he ran down the hallway he saw what looked like a classroom door on the right. He burst through the door to find a classroom full of children. His abrupt entrance startled Maria and the children. There were screams and some of the children began to cry.

"Please don't kill us," pleaded Maria.

"Don't be afraid! I'm not going to hurt you," responded Capt. Collins.

"Why are you here? What is it you want?" asked Maria.

"We believe an insurgent has planted a bomb in your school. You have to get out now!"

"Oh my God," Maria screamed, as the panic and fear among the children increased.

"Don't panic. Calm down. Line up single file and start moving out the door. Get as far away from the school as you can. Let's go, move!" Capt. Collins shouted.

"All right children, stay calm, do as he says, single file and out the door."

The children lined up and started moving quickly out the door, down the hall, and out the front door into the street.

Maria followed behind the children and urged them to keep moving quickly.

As the last child was leaving the classroom the Captain asked Maria, "Is there anyone else in the building?"

"No, this is the only class today," responded Maria.

"You get out with the rest of the children. I'll do a quick search to make sure there's no one else in the building."

Maria and the children had made it safely to the street while Capt. Collins checked the remaining classrooms. There were no more children and still no sign of the backpack. He ran to the restrooms to make sure there were no children left behind. First, he checked the girl's restroom. It was empty. He quickly moved over to the boy's restroom. No children, but there was the backpack. He didn't have his ordinance man with him, and had a bad feeling that time was running out, so he left the backpack and headed to the front door.

Just as he had cleared the front door, and made his way to the street, there was a tremendous explosion. The top of the roof over the restroom area was blown off, and the remaining section of the roof collapsed. Debris from the explosion was scattered over a wide area. The force of the blast had sent bricks flying though the air. One of those bricks had found Capt. Collins. As he tried to escape the blast, a brick hit him in the head knocking him off his feet.

Within minutes the street in front of the school was filled with people. Several of the theist sympathizers claimed the US soldier had tried to blow up the school. As the crowed gathered around the unconscious Captain, a pickup truck pulled up and two insurgents jumped out. They quickly grabbed Capt. Collins, threw him into the back of the truck and sped off. Maria had tried to make her way through the mob to explain what had happened, but it was too late.

While Capt. Collins was being taken by the insurgents, the rest of the Ranger team had troubles of their own. They had chased the insurgent to an apartment complex a few blocks from the school. The suspect entered the gates of the apartment complex with the Rangers hot on his heels. As they entered the gate after him, they came under small arms fire. The Rangers took cover in the alleyway inside the gates and returned fire. The insurgents had stopped firing. For a brief moment there was silence.

Sgt. Carpenter heard a thud, followed by the crack of a rifle. As he turned toward the direction of the thud, he saw Pfc. Benson fall to the ground. A snipers bullet had hit him in the neck.

"Sniper, get down," he yelled.

The Ranger standing next to Benson saw the reflection of the sunlight on the snipers scope. The sniper was on the top floor of the apartment building shooting out of an open window. Without hesitation the Ranger opened fire on the window sending glass and concrete flying. Again there was silence. Then the other insurgents began firing. Heavy incoming fire from the top floor of the apartment building pinned down the rangers trapping them in the street below. With the firefight raging, Sgt. Carpenter radioed for air support.

Within minutes the drone of the Apache AH-64E helicopter could be heard. As the Apache came in towards the apartment building its 30mm automatic cannon began firing, destroying the top floor of the apartment building and killing the insurgents. Once pass was all that was required, the firefight was over.

Prisoner of War

Capt. Collins was starting to regain consciousness. At first, he felt a tingling sensation throughout his body. Then, as his eyes flickered open and he tried to focus, he saw a harsh light emanating from a dark gray ceiling. He was flat on his back, and he felt as if his head was going to explode. Finally, back in the realm of consciousness, he attempted to determine where he was. The last thing he remembered was running out to the street from the school and hearing a large explosion. He was fortunate to be alive. Although his helmet was designed to deflect bullets, it apparently worked with bricks as well.

After lying on his back for what seemed to be hours, he finally felt as though he could sit up. As he sat up the pressure on his throbbing head intensified. He sat up and tried to orient himself to his new surroundings. He was feeling a bit queasy and decided to stay seated until he felt better. As he observed his surroundings it became obvious that he was in some sort of cell. The walls were a dull gray cobblestone. The floor was a dirty gray concrete. There was a single steel door with a small rectangular window about three quarters of the way up the door.

He heard a noise coming from outside his cell. First, there was the slamming of a door. Then he heard footsteps and voices outside his cell followed by what sounded like the unlocking of his cell door. The door swung open and two masked men dressed in black with AK-47 assault rifles entered the cell. One of the men pointed his gun at Capt. Collins while the other man grabbed him and yanked him to his feet. The guard put his arms behind his back and put handcuffs on him. Then they shoved him forward toward the open door. At the end of the hall they came to a set of stairs. It appeared that he was in the cellar of an old monastery. They went up the stairs and through another door that led to another hallway. At the end of the hallway he could see sunlight filtering through what appeared to be the front door of the building. There were several rooms on both sides of the hall. Midway down the hall they entered what looked like an interrogation room. The guards led him in the room and sat him down on a solid wooden chair. The interrogation room was stark. The walls were gray and empty of any pictures or decoration. The floor was gray concrete with no rugs or carpet. The only other items in the room were a plain wooden table and the interrogators plush executive office chair. At first, the ceiling light shined so brightly into his face that the interrogator appeared as a mere shadow. As his eyes got used to the light he could make out a big burly man with a beard wearing what appeared to be military fatigues or camouflage.

"Let's get started, shall we," the interrogator said in broken English. He motioned to the guards and said, "Bring in the equipment." Then he turned his attention back to Capt. Collins. "You know Capt. Collins; I am the sort of person who likes to get straight to the point. Here, I am the law. There are no rights. You have to answer our questions. Here, there are those who live and there are those who die. It is your choice."

The interrogator paused for a moment then he said, "Now tell me, why did you blow up that school?"

"My name is Jake Collins, my rank is Captain in the United States Army, and my serial number is 75766331, and I didn't try to blow up the school. I tried to save the children."

"But we have witnesses who saw you running from the school right before the explosion."

"After I got everyone else out, I tried to get out myself."

The interrogator looked up as the guards returned with the equipment cart. They rolled the cart up next to the desk and returned to their positions in front of the door. Capt. Collins glanced over at the equipment cart. On the cart there was a cattle prod, a piece of hickory that looked like an axe handle, pliers and a scalpel, some long needles, a soldering iron, and what appeared to be a small generator. He knew right away that things were going to get nasty.

"What is your mission?" asked the interrogator.

"My name is Jake Collins, my rank is Captain in the United States Army, and my serial number is 75766331."

"Where is the rest of your team?"

"I don't know. We got split up after the explosion."

"You are of no value to us. We did not sign the Geneva Convention. You are not a prisoner of war, you are a war criminal, and if you don't cooperate with us you will be executed."

The interrogator paused, lit a cigarette and continued, "Perhaps some additional time in your cell will improve your memory. Guards take this war criminal back to his cell." The first interrogation session had ended. The guards escorted him back to his cell to think things over.

Although he was spared from the interrogators equipment this time, he knew that it would not be long before they started using their tools on him. After his first interrogation, he knew he was either going to be executed or held captive for a very long time. His only chance of survival was to escape.

The next morning he started the day off by walking off the distances between the walls. The cell was a fifteen by fifteen feet square. He estimated the ceiling height to be ten feet. There were no windows so his only way out would have to be through the solitary door. Next, he checked out the door to see if there was any possibility of taking the door of its hinges. As he studied the door he heard the guards coming. He ran back and sat on his bed. The guards entered the cell and placed a bowl of rice and a canteen of water on the floor.

"Enjoy. It will probably be your last," the guard taunted.

By this time Jake was incredibly hungry and thirsty. He had not been given any water or food since his capture. He took a sip from the canteen. The cool water seemed like the best drink he had ever had. Then he scooped a handful of rice out of the bowl and ate it. He drank some more water but didn't finish it. It could be a long time before he would see any more.

After his food and water he felt much better and the throbbing pain in his head had begun to subside. He decided he needed to get some exercise to keep up his strength. He would have to keep his mind and body active if he were going to survive a long period of solitary confinement. Isolation has a tendency to beat you down. Even hardened criminals display fear at being moved to distant isolated areas, with no familiar surroundings, and no chance to see or hear from friends or relatives.

After walking off the dimensions of his cell he determined that there was just enough space to perform the Tae Kwon Do forms. Martial arts forms are standard movements that simulate fighting with multiple opponents, and are used in testing for advancement to higher belts. After completing his initial stretching, he would begin with Taegeuk Il Jang, which was the first form and work his way up to the black belt form Koryo. As he practiced his forms he fondly remembered the days of his youth when he first started taking Tae Kwon Do and broke his first board. It felt good to get some exercise and clear his mind for the task of preparing an escape plan. It had been silent the rest of the day. No guards came to his cell. No more food or water. As night fell, Jake started thinking about his team and home.

The interrogators know that the human mind craves routine and they do everything they can to disrupt or disable any semblance of routine. Sometimes the questioning would be loud and rough, while at other times it could be quiet and friendly, with no apparent reason for either. They would ask the same questions over and over again, then out of nowhere they would change subjects and act like they had the information they needed.

The next morning, Jake awoke to the sounds of the guards unlocking his cell door. It was time for another interrogation session. The guards delivered him to the interrogator who began another session.

"I trust you are feeling better, and are now ready to answer our questions. What is your mission?"

"My name is Jake Collins, my rank is Captain in the United States Army, and my serial number is 75766331."

"Why did you blow up that school?"

"I didn't blow up the school. I tried to save the children."

"Where is the rest of your team?"

"I don't know. We got split up after the explosion."

"Where is your camp?"

"I don't know"

"What is your next target?"

"I don't know."

The interrogator was clearly getting aggravated and walked around his desk and stood in front of Capt. Collins.

"Who were the other conspirators?"

"There were no conspirators."

The interrogator had enough, and with a swift back fist across the face, knocked him out of his chair. Then he set the guards on him. As he lay on the ground the guards kicked him several times, then the interrogator intervened and pulled them off. He pulled the Captain to his feet, put him back in his chair, and offered him a cigarette. Since the captain didn't smoke he declined. As the questioning continued a gunshot rang out, followed by another. The interrogator calmly said, "There is nothing to worry about; that was just the execution of another prisoner who refused to cooperate with us. I'm sure you will change your mind and cooperate with us so you do not suffer the same fate."

Groggy and in pain, the captain replied, "I have told you all I know."

"We will speak again tomorrow before the execution." The interrogator motioned to the guards and said, "Take him back to his cell."

Later that night the guards brought Jake some more rice and water and told him that this would be his last meal. As the guards left the cell, one of them turned around and pointed his rifle at Jake. Instead of shooting him the guard calmly said, "I will see you tomorrow for the execution."

Deployment to Turkey

For many families in the United States the fighting in Turkey had hit close to home. Kyle had already lost friends in the conflict, and he knew that more of his friends and neighbors would be injured or killed. For Kyle, it had been a whirlwind of activity since he met Ashley. He had fallen in love, got married and gone on his honeymoon all in less than two months time. Everything was like a blur. The wedding was a quick civil ceremony and the honeymoon was a weekend on Sanibel Island, Florida. Then it was back to reality.

His deployment to Turkey was only two weeks away so Kyle got his affairs in order. He updated his will and power of attorney form, and purchased a life insurance policy. He expected to be coming back, but he wanted to make sure that Ashley was taken care of in case he didn't return. There are no certainties in war.

Kyle and Ashley had talked about being in the military and the sacrifices that come with the job. Ashley understood what it would take to be married to an Air Force Pilot. Until she met Kyle, at this stage in her life, she never expected that she would be married and getting ready to see her husband off to war.

The weeks before Kyle's departure had been hectic and seemed to fly by. The final weekend before deployment had arrived. Kyle and Ashley, and Henry and Anne, decided to go out for a final dinner together before they shipped out. They settled on one of their favorite restaurants that had an all you can eat seafood buffet every Saturday night.

The seafood buffet was Kyle's favorite. They had piles of juicy tender crab legs with melted butter and lemon juice, shrimp, salmon, fried catfish, fried shrimp, and fried grouper. To top it all off, they had the best key lime pie to be found anywhere. By the time they were finished they were so stuffed they could barely move. They decided it might be a good idea to walk off some their dinner so they headed down to the beach for a walk and to view one final sunset.

When they arrived at the beach they decided to take pictures of each other so that Kyle and Henry would have a picture of them and their sweethearts to take to Turkey. It would be the closet thing to home they would have until they returned from their mission. They watched the orange red sun vanish below the horizon behind streaks of brightly colored purple and pink clouds painted across the brilliant blue sky. It was so beautiful, so peaceful, and so calm and quiet, the war seemed like it was light years away. They had one more drink, a toast to each other, and to the success of their mission, and then went home to have one final night alone before they had to leave for Turkey.

Monday came around far too quickly. The day of departure, the day everyone dreaded, had arrived. Kyle and Henry packed up their gear and left for Tyndall Air Force Base. The girls were going to meet them at the base so they could ride back together.

The laughter of children filled the air, friends and relatives shook hands and hugged each other, and a few people could be seen crying. It could have been a wedding or a family reunion, but instead the crowd had gathered to see the men and women of the 325th Fighter Wing off on their mission in support of Operation Unity. A brass band played patriotic songs as the American flags flapped in the breeze. The Commander gave a final speech commending the men and women for their service, their patriotism, and their courage.

"Today, we pause with you and your families at the dawn of a new era for humanity and a new mission, to honor your service to our nation and to thank you for answering your country's call to duty. As they serve with honor and distinction, the brave men and women of the 325th Fighter Wing are a reflection of America's best and brightest. We applaud the heroic work they do and acknowledge their families, friends and colleagues who support them."

"We understand that military service is unlike any other undertaking, your commitment to service and duty is nothing short of inspirational. We are confident in your abilities, in your training, and in your character. You are the finest soldiers in the world, the American soldier."

"We recognize the difficult road that lies ahead and the sacrifices made by you, your families, and your loved ones, and we pledge our support to the families you leave behind. And let me say a special word of encouragement to the family members with us today. Your loved one is a special breed of American charged with the most sacred of duties: ensuring that freedom, security, and prosperity are available to all. The pain of separation is real. While you will miss them dearly while they are gone, know that they are fulfilling a duty upon which the very future of civilization depends. In closing, I want to commend you for your willingness to serve, and your devotion to your fellow man. We salute you, and we thank you."

With the end of the speech and a final salute the ceremony ended. The crowd shared a final tearful goodbye as the airman gathered their belongings and prepared to depart.

"Be careful, be safe, and come back soon," said Ashley

Kyle, with a tear in his eye said, "Don't worry about me. You be careful and take care of yourself. I love you."

Ashley and Kyle enjoyed their final embrace, and a final kiss. Kyle turned and walked toward the runway. For a brief moment, a moment that seemed like an eternity, Ashley stood alone and watched as Kyle climbed into the cockpit of his F-35EX. The engines roared to life. As he taxied down the runway to prepare for take off, he turned his head for one last look and saw his beautiful Ashley. He flashed her a thumbs-up and put his visor down. Ashley waved and started to cry as Kyle soared off the runway, his shimmering aircraft disappearing into the deep blue sky.

Time for Tea

As the fighting intensified in Turkey, it was time for the second meeting between the Commander and the Librarian. The guard escorted the Librarian into the Commander's office. The Commander was standing in front of his bookshelves reviewing a book on military history when they came in. The guard led the Librarian over to a small conference table and chairs.

"Please, sit down professor. Would you like to join me for a cup of tea?" asked the Commander.

"Yes, a cup of tea would be very nice. I do miss my afternoon tea," replied the Librarian.

The commander poured the Librarian and himself a cup of tea and returned to the table and sat down.

"You have quite a library Commander," said the Librarian.

"Reading is one of the greatest pleasures of life," replied the Commander.

"Yes, it is. I especially enjoy books on archeology and papyrology. My favorites are the Greek Papyri."

"Professor, do you remember when the first religious war occurred?"

"Some would say the Maccabean revolt against the Seleucid overlords of Judea in 165 BC was the first truly religious war, although the war between the Sumerians and the Elamites around 2700 BC is considered to be the first documented war."

"I think most scholars would agree with you that the Maccabean revolt was the first religious war. Why do you think that over 2000 years later we are still at war over religion?"

"People have always fought for what they believe in. They are fighting for the freedom to worship their God or gods as they see fit."

"The fighting is not about freedom of worship, it is about the imposition of one religion over another and the superiority of one self-proclaimed true religion over another. This was true during the Crusades and it is true today."

"I cannot defend the Crusades. But there are many who do not believe in conversion and violence, or that they are the sole keepers of the truth. They just want to be left alone to worship and pray in peace."

"I am afraid it is too late for them. The endless cycle of death and destruction will be stopped."

"This war is not the way to accomplish human tranquility. It will only perpetuate the cycle of violence."

"There is no other way. The fire of hate must be extinguished once and for all, or the cycle will never end."

There was a knock on the door. It was one of the guards.

"I'm sorry to interrupt Sir, but General Anderson is here to see you."

"Thank you Ensign."

"Well professor, it looks like we're going to have to continue this discussion next week. There are many fields of knowledge I would like to discuss with you. Perhaps we could have weekly meetings. What do you think about meeting every Tuesday at 1500 hours for afternoon tea?"

"Yes, I would like that."

The Librarian stood up and the guard escorted him back to his cell.

Deception in the Ranks

In the military, as in most large organizations, there is always one bad apple that gives the rest of the organization a bad name. Sgt. Johnny Parker was one of those bad apples. He was always quick to blame someone else for his mistakes, and equally quick to claim credit for other peoples work. He had a knack for making himself look good with the least amount of effort, and would never pass up the chance to make a quick buck.

It was the end of another long day and Sgt. Johnny Parker was looking forward to his two-day leave the following week. The first thing he was going to do, was go out and get a great big steak and an ice cold beer, and then head out on the town to see what kind of female companionship he could find. He had talked to some of his buddies, and they were all heading over to their standard hangout, the Nexus Lounge. There were usually a lot of great looking women there, and they loved men in uniform.

Sgt. Parker's big weekend finally arrived, it was time to party. He arrived at the Nexus Lounge early, hoping to get a good seat at the bar. He found an empty seat, bellied up to the bar, and ordered a cold beer. He took a few swigs off his beer and started checking the place out. He still didn't see any of his buddies, but at the other end of the bar he spotted something even better. There sat one of the most beautiful redheads he had ever seen. He gazed at her for a brief moment, and had another sip of beer. She appeared to be alone, but seemed to be disinterested in her surroundings. At first, he thought she might hang too high on the tree for him. After all, Johnny was in his forties, with balding brownish gray hair, more than a couple pounds overweight, and by most peoples reckoning not a very engaging conversationalist.

Despite the obvious age difference, and lacking in physical attributes, he couldn't resist. He gathered his courage and decided to walk over to where she was sitting. He slid in between the solitary beauty and the person in the next seat, and ordered another beer. As he flagged down the bartender he glanced over at the young lady who was now looking at him.

"I was just getting ready to order another beer, may I buy you a drink?" he asked.

"I usually don't drink with strangers," she replied.

"I understand, ma'am," replied Sgt. Parker.

"However, I do support the military, so I suppose I can make an exception."

With that the Sergeant started beaming and asked, "What'll you have?"

"I would like a Macallan on the rocks, please," replied Angela.

The bartender came over to take his order. "Yeah bartender, the lady will have a Macallan on the rocks, and I'll have a Budweiser in the bottle."

"What's Macallan?" Sgt. Parker asked the young lady.

"Some of the finest single malt scotch that Scotland has to offer. Eighteen years in those sherry seasoned Spanish oak casks," she replied.

The bartender delivered their drinks and said, "That'll be $25.00 please."

Twenty five dollars for two drinks on a sergeant's salary was a little more than he bargained for.

"Wow that stuffs not cheap! It must be the finest scotch in Scotland," said the surprised Sergeant.

"The finer brands of single malt scotch can get quite expensive," commented the young woman.

As he extended his hand to shake hands with the young lady he said, "I'm sorry, I didn't even introduce myself; I'm Chief Master Sergeant Johnny Parker, at your service!"

"My name is Angela Kibble; it's a pleasure to meet you Sergeant."

"You sound like you're from Britain."

"Yes, I am. I live in London, but I'm here on business."

"What kind of business are you in?"

"I am a barrister. How about you Sergeant, where are you from?"

Never missing a chance to brag about his position and inflate his importance, Johnny replied, "I'm based at MacDill Air Force Base, here in Tampa. I am in charge of all logistics for the US Central Command."

"That sounds like a big job."

"Yeah, it's big all right. It keeps us hopping."

"I'll bet you are really busy now that we are at war."

"We can barely keep up with the troops they're moving so fast."

Angela finished her drink and prepared to leave when Sgt. Parker asked, "I was supposed to meet some of my buddies here, but it doesn't look like their going to show up. What do you say, would you like another drink?"

"I'm sorry, Sergeant. I have an early morning meeting tomorrow and only have time for one drink."

Disappointed he replied, "I understand."

"But you seem very nice. I'm in the States quite often for business. Perhaps next time I'm in Tampa, you can show me around."

He could hardly believe his ears and with obvious excitement exclaimed, "That would be fantastic!"

"How can I reach you?" asked Angela.

"Here is my card. I would be happy to show you the sites, anytime."

With that Angela stood up, finished her drink and said, "Thanks for the drink Sergeant; I will give you a call the next time I'm in the states."

"It was a pleasure to meet you. I can't wait to show you around."

"It was a pleasure to meet you as well, goodbye Sergeant."

As Angela walked out of the bar, all Sergeant Parker could do was stand in amazement as he watched her leave. His buddies were never going to believe him.

The following week it was back to the grind for Sgt. Parker. He had just received orders to ship additional supplies to Turkey, and arrange for a shipment of weapons and ammunition from Turkey to Mosul in northern Iraq. Here was his chance to try out his new system for making a little extra money. He wasn't ready to start selling weapons to the black marketers, but he didn't have any problem selling food and equipment. With the quantities of supplies the military went through, he didn't think anyone would miss a few crates of supplies.

The scheme worked by entering the original order, then making adjustments to the order after the shipping paperwork had already been generated. This particular order consisted of 100 crates of food, 25 crates of medicine, 10 crates of tents, and 5 crates of first aid kits. For the 100 crates of food he entered 106 crates, for the 25 crates of medicine and medical supplies he entered 30 crates, for the 10 crates of tents he entered 14 crates, and for the 5 crates of first aid kits he entered 7 crates. Once the entries were complete he printed the shipping paperwork for removal from the warehouse and shipment to Turkey. He then went back into the system, and adjusted the number of crates back to the original order amounts.

His accomplice worked at Incirlik Air Base in Turkey, the shipment's destination. From there the shipment would be split up and trucked to the forces in the field. His accomplice would receive the full order and place the over shipped crates in a separate holding area where they were supposed to be picked up and shipped to another base. Instead of shipping them to another base, he would call his middleman in Turkey, and arrange for him to do the pick up.

They would then sell the goods to the Turkish middleman for $7,000. Sgt Parker would get $5,000 and his accomplice would get $2,000. The Turkish middleman could turn around and sell the food and equipment for well over $15,000, so everyone was happy. Johnny had just completed the deal when the phone rang. It was Angela Kibble.

"Sgt. Parker, this is Angela, we met at the Nexus Lounge."

"Angela, I could never forget you. How are you?"

"I'm well thank you. I am going to be in town next weekend and you mentioned something about showing me around next time I was in town."

"Yeah, that would be great; I'd love to show you around."

Johnny gave her directions to his favorite steakhouse, and told her he would meet her there at 7:00 PM Saturday night. It was like a dream come true. He couldn't believe that a beautiful woman like Angela actually called him back for a date.

The day of Johnny's big date finally arrived. Johnny got to the steakhouse early. He didn't want to take any chances that Angela might not see him and leave. Getting a date, any date, was special for Johnny, but a date with a girl like Angela was a once in a lifetime opportunity. Johnny was sitting at the bar when he saw Angela walk in. She was even hotter then he remembered. He quickly approached her.

"Hello Sergeant," she said.

"Hi Angela, you don't have to be so formal, just call me Johnny."

"Okay Johnny, are you hungry?"

"Yeah, I'm always hungry. Our table is ready."

They walked over and sat down at their table. Johnny, being on his best behavior, pulled Angela's chair out for her and made sure she was seated before he sat down.

"You still drinking that single malt scotch?" asked Johnny.

"Still drinking the Macallan," she replied.

They ordered drinks and a couple of steaks, and Angela started throwing out some questions to Johnny in an attempt to size him up.

"So how is the logistics business?" asked Angela.

"It's been brutal. With the war and everything its just non-stop," he replied.

"What do you think about the war? Do you believe in the cause?" asked Angela.

"I don't think much about it either way. Its just more work to me."

As Angela took another sip of scotch she thought to herself, here is man with no allegiance.

"How about you, what have you been up to?" asked Johnny.

"Unfortunately, too much travel. I barely have time to unpack when I get called to go somewhere else and have to pack and leave again."

"That would be hard. With all the security checks and the mismanaged airlines travel can be a real nightmare."

"Yes, it does get a bit old. I don't even have time to go out on dates. I get lonely sometimes."

Finding a lonely woman with no boyfriend, now that was music to Johnny's ears. He was just the man to bring some excitement into her life.

Working in the British Foreign Office required a great deal of travel. There was little time to establish any long-term relationships. Angela was a very lonely woman, spending her life in lonely hotel rooms, staring out of hotel room windows and seeing people everywhere, couples arm in arm, but still feeling alone. She was often separated from familiar people and places, and felt disconnected. She tried to compensate for her feelings of loneliness by working long hours, hoping the concentration on work would mask the painful feelings of desolation. But she could not escape the persistent shadow of loneliness and the emptiness that she felt. She drank her cherished Macallan hoping it would dull her senses and help her sleep. The first few drinks made her feel better, but the more she drank the lonelier she became.

They finished dinner and were getting ready to head out the door when Johnny asked, "Why don't we go back to my place for a nightcap? I even have a bottle of Macallan?"

"I have a meeting in the morning, but since you got a bottle of my favorite scotch, I guess I could come by for one more Macallan to insure a good nights' sleep."

They headed back to Johnny's house. Johnny got another beer and poured Angela a glass of Macallan and took a seat on the couch. It didn't take Angela long to swing into action.

"Why don't you try a shot of Macallan?" she asked.

"I don't usually drink much whiskey," said Johnny.

"Oh come on, just one shot. Where's a shot glass?"

Not wanting to disappoint Angela, and unable to say no he gave in, "Well, I guess I could try just one."

Johnny got up and got a shot glass out of the cabinet. He brought the shot glass and the bottle of Macallan back to the table. Angela poured him a shot, handed him the glass and said, "Bottoms up!"

Johnny slammed back the shot and made a face, but he was pleasantly surprised at how mild the Macallan was.

"Not bad," he said.

"I told you that Macallan is good stuff. It's the best. You better have another," she said as she poured him another shot.

"I heard on the news, that there are a lot of troops heading over to Turkey," she said.

"Yeah, I guess Turkey's a big deal right now. We just sent more stuff over there today."

"What kind of stuff?"

"Oh, you know the usual, supplies, arms and ammunition, that kind of stuff."

Several shots later Angela had him were she wanted him. The Macallan had achieved its desired effect. Johnny was flat on his back. Angela straddled him, lowered her shapely hips down on him, and began to grind. Intoxicated with drink and lust he quickly succumbed to her charms.

"Now about that arms shipment, what was that route again?" she asked with an evil smile.

As the seductive Angela worked him into a state of hypnotic euphoria, he was helpless in her hands as he told her the details of the arms shipment.

She finished her dirty work and rolled off him. For a moment she thought about killing him, but decided that he may be useful in the future, and let him live for now. Johnny was spent from sex and drink and quickly passed out.

Angela had the information she wanted and returned to her hotel room. She poured herself a Macallan on the rocks and sat down in front of her notebook computer. She connected to the Internet and went to a website called travelforum.com. Travelforum.com was a website where people could post travel information and their personal travel experiences. Angela logged into the website using her anonymous account name 'Bold Angel.' Once logged in, she proceeded to enter the following:

> *On my latest trip to Turkey and Iraq I had a great time. The best route between Silopi in Southeast Turkey and Mosul in Northern Iraq is via Highway 2. I usually go there around August 12th because the weather is so lovely at the time of the year. Since there are often afternoon storms the best time to travel is between 9:00AM and 1:00 PM.*

Her drop completed, she leaned back in her chair and finished her glass of Macallan. Angela had used a technique that became popular with terrorists back in the early part of the century for communicating information about planned terrorist strikes. Posting hidden, sometimes encrypted messages inside other messages had been used for decades by criminal organizations and terrorist networks. They would hide maps, photographs, messages about targets, and post instructions for carrying out terrorist acts on chat rooms, pornographic websites, and various blogger sites on the Internet. These messages have the same characteristics as a dead drop in that the two parties are never seen together, they don't have to coordinate a rendezvous point, and one party doesn't even have to know the identity of the other party, which is a definite advantage if one of them is captured. This method also works well with the cell type organizational structure that is used by most modern revolutionary and terrorist movements.

Cell structured organizations are formed by dividing a larger organization into multiple smaller groups or cells. By compartmentalizing information inside each cell as needed, the organization is more likely to survive if one of its components is compromised. The functional areas of the cells are usually divided into planning, sleeper, and execution cells. In some cases, operational commanders may be sent in at the last moment to coordinate an attack.

The next morning, Johnny woke up in a fog with a splitting headache. Angela was nowhere to be found. With his alcohol clouded mind, he had a difficult time remembering the events of the previous night, but from the intensity of his hangover, he figured he must of had a good time.

Angela and the President

After weeks of effort, Angela had finished her work, and was ready to present the Middle Eastern re-education plans at a meeting with the President scheduled for 8:00 PM that evening. The purpose of the meeting with the President was to finalize the plans for rebuilding the schools, establishing the re-education camps, and re-educating the people of the defeated nations. For the long-term success of the war effort it was critical that the re-education programs were implemented quickly and effectively. President Adams had a personal stake in the success of the re-education plans. If the re-education plans failed, and the minds of the masses were not cleansed of their primitive beliefs, the war would end in failure.

Angela looked terrific as usual. She was wearing a dark blue jacket with a form fitting white cashmere sweater and dark blue pants. With her curled hair, black-rimmed glasses, and briefcase she appeared to be all business. Upon arriving at the White House, a Secret Service agent escorted her to the Oval Office.

The Oval Office is the President's formal workspace, where he confers with heads of state, diplomats, his staff, and other dignitaries, and where he often addresses the American public and the world on television and radio. The Oval Office has four doors: the east door opens to the Rose Garden; the west door leads to the President's private kitchen and study; the northwest door opens onto the main corridor of the West Wing; and the northeast door opens to the President's personal secretary's office.

Angela entered the Oval office and greeted the President, "Good evening Mr. President."

"Good evening Ms. Kibble how are you tonight?"

"Very well, thank you."

"May I take your jacket?"

"Yes, thank you."

"Where is the Foreign Secretary?" asked the President.

"Nigel became ill after lunch and could not join us. He wanted you to know that he was sorry he could not attend the meeting but felt we should meet anyway. I hope you're not disappointed."

"No, certainly not, I am sorry to hear about Nigel, I hope he feels better soon."

Angela removed her jacket. As she removed her jacket and handed it to the President he could not help but notice what a fine figure she had. The last time he had seen her was in an evening gown at the reception. As he hung up her jacket he said, "I understand you have completed the plans for the British role in the re-education phase of the project. I'm eager to review and approve them, so we can move forward with implementation."

"Yes, Mr. President. I have the project plan right here. I believe we have covered all the project tasks and defined a realistic timeline. We have also included risk probabilities and contingency plans in case there are problems with the initial implementation."

Angela opened up her briefcase and pulled out the report.

"Why don't we work over here at the conference table?" the President said as he guided Angela over to the table. As she walked over to the table his eyes were instinctively drawn to her tight shapely posterior. He couldn't help but wonder if her walk was genetic or learned behavior.

Angela began to review the plans with the President and said, "Mr. President, I don't suppose you have any single malt scotch handy do you?"

"Yes, I believe we do my apologies for not offering you something to drink."

The President walked into the study where several bottles of spirits, sodas and an ice bucket where kept.

"It looks like all we have is the Glenlivet 18-year-old, will that do?"

"Yes, that would be very nice, thank you."

"How would you like that?"

"Straight up on ice would be wonderful."

The President returned to the conference table and handed the drink to Angela.

"Aren't you going to join me?" asked Angela.

"I would like to, but I have a rule, I never consume alcohol until my work is done for the day."

"You are a disciplined man Mr. President."

As she sat back down at the conference table and took a sip from her drink she asked, "Mr. President, do you really think that through these programs you can win the hearts and minds of the people after destroying their religion."

"We are destroying the foundation of division and hate. The cleansing program and the re-education initiative have to work. If they don't, our efforts will have failed, and in five years we will be back at war."

"It will take time to erase the memories of the people," Angela commented.

"If we can improve people's standard of living and quality of life, the old memories will fade. We are going to make the functioning of schools and the rebuilding of infrastructure our top priority. It is our responsibility to help these people, and to educate them, so they can get good jobs and provide for their families. Our goal is to improve their lives, not add to their misery."

"What about the spiritual needs of the people during the transition?" Angela asked.

"With real material progress such as better health care, food and nutrition, and housing, the need for spiritual want will decrease," replied the President.

Angela finished her drink, removed her glasses, and asked the President for another. The President stood up and walked back to the study. As the President was making her drink, Angela stood up and followed the President into the study, as she walked she removed her sweater. The President turned around and Angela moved closer to him, her firm breasts shimmering in the soft light.

"Mr. President, I think you are very handsome, and you get me very excited."

The President almost dropped her drink, so he put it down on the table.

"Angela, please stop," he pleaded.

"Don't you find me attractive?" she said with a sexy but sad expression.

"Yes, I think you are a very beautiful woman. But I'm a married man."

She moved closer and tried to kiss him.

"He gently placed his hands on her bare shoulders and said, "Please Angela, I made a promise to be faithful to my wife."

"No one will ever know. I want to be with you."

"I'm sorry Angela. I cannot break my vows."

Angela tried once again to kiss him, but he held her back.

"Please Angela, I think it is time for you to leave."

Angela started crying. She picked up her sweater, put it back on, gathered her things, and walked out the door. She had left her Middle Eastern re-education report on the table.

The President was bewildered at what had just transpired. Angela had always given the appearance of being a serious, dedicated diplomat. He never considered himself a ladies man or handsome. He loved his wife Elizabeth very much and would never do anything to harm her. He was a moral and disciplined man, as resisting the beautiful Angela had just confirmed.

The Escape

Jake was practicing his Tae Kwon Do forms, when he heard the guards approaching. The cell door opened, it was the teacher from the school. As she entered the cell, the guard shut the door behind her. Maria walked up to Jake, and slapped him across the face. As she slapped him with her right hand, she dropped a tightly folded note on the floor in front of him. After Maria slapped the prisoner's face the guard had seen enough and turned away to have a cigarette.

"What was that for?" asked Jake.

"I had to convince the guard," Maria replied.

"What is your name?"

"I am Maria Milionis."

"You are the daughter of the Archbishop?"

"Yes, but I'm afraid even he cannot spare your life. I have just come from meeting with my father. I tried to explain to him that you saved my life, but no one believes me. They are all convinced that you tried to destroy the school, so you are to be executed. You are being held in abandoned monastery in the mountains south of Trabzon. The note on the floor has directions to a lake where I have left you food, water, and clothes. It is all I can do."

"Thank you Maria."

"I must go." As she turned to leave she said, "Thank you for saving me and the children."

She knocked on the cell door, the guard let her out and she was gone. As Maria walked out Capt. Collins stepped on the note so the guard would not see it. After the guards left, he picked up the note and unfolded it. There was a map with directions to a small mountain lake, and the location of the supplies. From the lake, the map showed a trail that led out of the mountains down to the town of Uzungol, where he could catch a ride back to his camp. Now, all he had to do was to get out of the prison.

The next day, two guards came to take him to the interrogator. Today could be just another day of interrogation, or it could be execution day. Whether he was to be executed or just introduced to the interrogator's tools, Jake didn't want to stick around and find out. As the guards entered his cell, he grabbed the lead guard's rifle and pulled him to the right side of his body while executing a left front sliding sidekick to the guard's solar plexus. The kick landed with such force you could hear the guard's ribs snap, as he was sent reeling into the cell wall, the wind gone from his lungs. As the second guard began to raise his weapon, Jake turned quickly, and with a spinning heel kick caught the guard in the left temple and knocked him out. As the guard fell to the ground like a sack of potatoes, Jake quickly used the rifle butt to finish off the other guard. After killing the guards he grabbed the guard's survival knife, the key to the cell, and removed the ammunition clip from the other guard's rifle and put it in his pocket.

He moved quickly towards the open cell door. The hallway was clear. He locked the cell door on his way out, and made his way down the hall to the stairs. As he got to the top of the stairs he heard voices coming from the front of the building. He knew there were multiple guards in the front of the monastery so he went to the back door and looked out the small window in the door. He saw a single guard sitting on the outside edge of a thick stone wall. He wasn't too keen on the idea of starting a firefight without knowing exactly how many theist fighters there were. Instead, he decided to try and take out the guard at the rear of the monastery. He moved quietly out of the structure and towards the guard, hugging the wall as he went. When he got behind the guard, with the survival knife in his hand he used an out to in movement, and thrust the knife through the guard's temple into his brain killing him instantly. He vaulted over the wall and ran as fast as he could for the cover of the forest.

It was about a three hour hike down to the lake from the monastery. Jake followed the map Maria had given him to where she had stashed the supplies. Just off the path that circled the lake, there was another small path that led to a pile of rocks. He removed the rocks and found a canvas bag. He turned the bag over and emptied its contents.

There was a large bag of mixed nuts, a bar of dark chocolate, two bottles of water, a pack of matches, and a fleece jacket. Everything he would need to survive for several days in the mountains, if for some reason he could not make it down to Uzungol.

He opened the bag of nuts, grabbed a handful and ate them followed by a square of the dark chocolate. Then he washed the nuts and chocolate down with some water. For a man that had been living on rice and water, nuts and chocolate never tasted so good. His thirst quenched and feeling energized, he packed everything back into the canvas bag and headed back to the main trail. He new the insurgents would not be far behind, so he would have to keep moving.

It was about another four hours hike down to Uzungol where he had hoped to find a ride back to camp. When he got to the edge of the forest outside of Uzungol he scoped out the town to make sure there were no signs of the enemy. He moved towards the main road out of town, to see if he could commandeer a vehicle, and get a ride back down to Trabzon. Finally, he saw a car coming down the road. He jumped out into the road and pointed his AK47 at the driver. The car stopped and an old man got out with his hands up pleading for his life, "Please don't kill me. You can have the car," he pleaded.

"I'm not going to hurt you. I don't want your car. I just need a ride down to Trabzon," replied Jake.

The old man was suspicious, but fearing for his life, he had no choice but to do what he was told.

"Get back into the car, slowly," said Jake as he motioned to the old man to get back into the car. Jake quickly got into the passenger side of the car, keeping his gun pointed at the old man.

"Drive until I tell you to stop," said Jake. The old man did as he was told, and Jake was finally on his way back to camp and his Ranger team.

The sun was setting as Capt. Collins walked into the Ranger camp. His old friend Sgt. Carpenter ran up to him, hugged him, patted him on the shoulder and said, "I thought you were dead Sir."

"Not yet. How's the team?"

"We lost Benson, Sir. The same day you disappeared. We were going after the bomber, when we got ambushed and caught up in a firefight. Benson got hit by a sniper. He went down fighting."

"Damn! Benson was a superb soldier. We all loved him like a brother," Jake paused for a moment, and reflected on his time with Benson then he continued, "It's going to be difficult. But we all have to be strong for the team."

"Yes Sir, at least you made it back alive. By the way, where in the world have you been?"

"It's a long story. I'll tell you all about it tomorrow after I get some rest."

The next day was a busy one as the Ranger team went right back into action. The Ranger's seized a weapons cache in a town east of Trabzon. During the raid they seized about 400 rocket-propelled grenade (RPGs) launchers and rounds, 50 AK-47s and 1300 rounds of ammunition. The RPGs are the insurgent's weapons of choice. They are easy to fire, and can cause extensive damage.

On the way back to camp the patrol surprised insurgents placing explosives for a roadside bomb, and came under small arms fire. They killed two insurgents and seized explosives, 75 blasting caps, and 3 rolls of detonation cord.

Coalition forces continued aggressive patrols throughout Turkey. The patrols and raids had made a significant impact on the number and movement of the insurgents. Since the operation began the Rangers had conducted 75 raids and detained over 500 individuals, including 38 individuals identified as key insurgent leaders. Most of the insurgents had moved out of the area, and were reportedly heading down to the Islamic Front states for a final stand.

That night, things were unusually quiet. It was a beautiful clear night with the stars shinning brightly, and the planet Venus ascending over the horizon. For the moment there was no gunfire, no bombs, and no fighting. Jake and his friend Sgt. Carpenter could finally get some much-needed relaxation.

"You know Sir, this line of work wouldn't be so bad if people weren't trying to kill you all the time and there weren't so many damn insects," said Sgt. Carpenter.

"Yeah, you're right. When I was up in Alaska on a training mission one summer it was unbelievable. The mosquitoes were vicious and relentless. They would actually dive bomb you. There were billions of the filthy things. You had to have mosquito netting covering you head and every part of your body or they would swarm all over you, thousands of them biting you until you were covered with red welts. They were so bad, that when you were boiling water for coffee, they would swarm to the heat and fall by the hundreds into your pot. You had to try to lift up your mosquito netting and bring the cup of coffee up underneath the netting to take a drink or the mosquitoes would land in your cup or bite your face. Legend has it that a hunter stumbled across a caribou calf that had been sucked dry by a swarm of mosquitoes."

"I hate those filthy bloodsuckers," commented Sgt. Carpenter.

Jake continued, "Then there were the clouds of bloodthirsty black flies. They're sneaky little devils. They will crawl all over you until the find a good spot to start their meal. You would wake up with intensely itchy bites all over you that would last for weeks."

"You think that's bad," Sgt. Carpenter, countered, "When I was in South America on a mission, the mosquitoes would pick up botfly eggs, and when they bite you, they would deposit the eggs under your skin. In a few weeks, you would have this disgusting, oozing red dome on you, and you could feel this crawling sensation and a stinging pain. Well, it was the filthy spine covered larvae wiggling around under your skin. You would have to cover up their breathing hole to force the loathsome creatures out. Nasty! Then you had your bees and wasps, your black flies and sand flies, sand fleas, and of course those ugly spiders and scorpions. It makes a fellow never want to go out in the wilderness again."

"I can't take any more! I'm going to have bug nightmares if you keep this up. I'm hitting the sack."

Jake had heard enough about the insects of the world. He could handle just about anything but he hated bugs. He climbed into his tent, kicked of his boots and crawled into his sleeping bag. As Jake lay in his tent looking through the skylight at the brilliant stars, his mind drifted back to Maria. There was something about her that was unlike any woman he had ever met. Maybe it was her dark complexion, or her big brown eyes. Or maybe it was the way she slapped him in the cell. He wasn't sure what it was, but he wanted to see her again. He also wanted to thank her again for helping him escape, and maybe even saving his life.

The Lonely Journey Ends

The day started off as just another monotonous day of cleaning when the maid entered Room 255. As was customary, she knocked on the door to announce her arrival. There was no response. She knocked again, still no response. With no response, she assumed the room was empty, and she could enter to begin her work. As she entered the room, she noticed a woman who appeared to be sleeping in a chair in the corner of the room.

"Pardon me. I thought the room was empty. I didn't mean to disturb you," explained the maid.

There was no response from the woman in the chair. Believing that the woman was still sleeping, she prepared to leave the room when she noticed a bottle of whisky and a pill bottle on the table. She approached the woman to see if she was all right, and noticed that she didn't appear to breathing. The maid knew that something was wrong, and called emergency services.

She dialed 911 and said, "There is a woman up here, and she doesn't appear to be breathing, please send someone over. I am at the Renaissance Mayflower Hotel in Room 255, please hurry."

Within minutes the police and Emergency Medical Services (EMS) team arrived and entered the room. It was too late. The woman had apparently died from a drug overdose. As the police looked for identification, one of the officers found an open notebook that appeared to have fallen on the floor beside the dead woman. On the open page were the words, 'I have failed in my mission. Integrity and morals can exist in the godless. I can no longer endure.' As the detective was reading the notebook, one of the officers had found the dead woman's purse and wallet.

"Who is she?" asked the detective.

"Her name is Angela Kibble. She appears to be a British diplomat," replied the police officer.

"I'll contact the British embassy."

The detective contacted the British embassy and informed them of Angela's death. The British Ambassador to the United States immediately contacted Undersecretary Barnett and told him what had happened.

"Sir, I am sorry to inform you that US authorities have found Angela Kibble dead in her hotel room," said the Ambassador.

"That's bloody awful. You must get someone over there immediately and seal that hotel room," demanded Undersecretary Barnett.

"Yes Sir, I will dispatch a special agent immediately."

The special agent arrived at the hotel and went up to Angela's room. The police were still there carrying out their investigation. The special agent displayed his identification and said, "Detective, I am special agent Andrew Manning with the British Embassy. We need to seal this room immediately. This is a national security issue."

"We have just begun our investigation, nothing has been removed," replied the detective.

"What is your summation of the situation?" asked Special Agent Manning.

"It looks like an apparent suicide. We found this notebook next to her," he said as he handed Special Agent Manning the notebook with Angela's last words written in it.

"Very well detective, please finish your work. I will need to take her personal items and her computer with me when you have completed your investigation."

"Okay, it shouldn't take too much longer."

The police finished their investigation and Special Agent Manning collected Angela's possessions. Special Agent Manning returned to the British embassy and sent her personal items and computer to the security service laboratory for analysis.

Angela had died as she had lived, all alone in her final lonely hotel room. A cool and calculating exterior cloaked a troubled mind. She had found temporary salvation in Jesus and the bottle, but her tormented mind was unable to cope with the notion that the enemies of religion could be disciplined moral people with a noble cause.

The following day the President was reviewing the morning paper when the phone rang. A call was coming in from Undersecretary Barnett.

"Mr. President, this is Undersecretary Barnett with the Foreign Office."

"Yes Nigel, how are you?"

"Not very well today Sir," he replied.

"Oh, what's the problem?"

"Well Sir, we have discovered a spy operating in the Foreign Office. It was Angela Kibble. A maid discovered her body in her hotel room yesterday. It appears that she took her own life."

"That explains the other night," the President mumbled.

"What was that Sir?"

"Oh nothing, has anything been compromised?"

"We are still analyzing her computer for evidence. We did find one thing. The name Angela Kibble, means 'Bold Angel.' She was apparently working for the theists."

"I suggest you do a thorough review. Please keep me informed of any further developments."

"Yes Sir, Mr. President."

The President thought how sad it was, that such an intelligent and beautiful woman could have been so distraught and depressed that she would take her own life.

The Search for Maria

Capt. Collins drove back into town to where Maria's old school had been. As he gazed at the rubble where the school had once stood, he noticed an old man picking up bricks, and placing them in a wheelbarrow. He approached the old man to see if he could help him find Maria. When the old man saw the soldier approaching he became frightened and looked around for a way out. As the old man began to run away Jake caught up with him, grabbed him by the arm and said, "Please. Stop! I'm not going to hurt you. I'm looking for Maria Milionis. Where can I find her?"

In a trembling voice the old man said, "Since the school was destroyed, she is holding class at the Anatolia Café."

Jake let go of the man's arm and thanked him for his help. He drove over to the Anatolia Café and parked out front. He walked in the front door of the café. There was a seating area in the front part of the building with wooden chairs and tables covered with dark red tablecloths. On one wall there was a large portrait of Ataturk. To his right was a young woman standing behind a counter. He approached the young woman and said, "I'm looking for Maria Milionis. I understand she is here."

Startled but helpful, the young lady pointed to the door, which led to the banquet rooms. He entered the banquet room, which had been turned into a makeshift classroom. There was Maria at the front of the room writing a math problem on the blackboard. As she turned from the blackboard she saw him standing in the back of the room.

For a moment she froze. She had not expected to see Capt. Collins again. She told the children to continue working on the problem. She walked through the tables of children towards Jake as the children's eyes followed her to the back of the room.

"Maria, I'm sorry to interrupt your class, but I had to see you. I wanted to thank you again for helping me. Without your help I probably wouldn't have survived."

"I did very little. It was the least I could do after you saved my life and the children."

"How are the children?"

"They are fine. We are holding classes here at the café until we can build a new school."

"I'm happy to hear that the children are well."

Then in a more serious tone Jake asked Maria, "Why haven't the townspeople turned the bomber over to the authorities?"

"They are afraid. They don't want to be seen supporting the enemy," replied Maria.

"How can you still support these people? They tried to kill you and the children?"

"They're fighting for their beliefs."

With a scornful tone Jake responded, "That's the problem. Their beliefs are erroneous. They don't care about truth, justice, or reason. They are killing innocent people. They tried to kill you!"

"You are killing people because of their faith."

"No, we are killing the enemies of reason."

"Only love can bring the world together, not hate and war," said Maria.

"Love is not a weapon. You can't use love when a person will kill you because you are not of the same faith, or simply because you're an American," responded Jake.

"You are our enemy, but you risked your life to save our children. And you saved me," countered Maria.

"But it wasn't for love. It was just the right thing to do," calming down Jake continued, "But if I hadn't gone into that school, I would never have met you."

Maria was attracted to Jake, and considered him an honorable man. He had saved her life and the lives of her children. For that she would always be grateful. But she knew that to continue to see him would be very dangerous for both of them.

"I must get back to the children," said Maria.

"May I see you again?" asked Jake.

"I'm sorry. I don't think that would be a good idea. Goodbye Captain."

Jake stood and watched Maria as she returned to the front of the room. When she reached the front of the room, she looked at him once more, then turned back to the blackboard and continued the lesson. Jake left the café and returned to camp. On the drive back all he could think about was Maria. With her long brown hair, and trim curvaceous figure, she had an exotic appearance that fascinated him. It was a pity that she was so misguided. He couldn't understand how she could continue to support the very people who tried to kill her.

Resistance Eliminated

It was a clear cold night in the Rocky Mountains of Colorado. With a new moon, the sky was dark except for the brilliant stars. Jack Cody and eight of his men had setup camp midway up a canyon next to a mountain stream. The fire was slowly burning down with the smoke drifting down the canyon, as the men prepared to turn in for the night.

On the other side of the ridge, two helicopters flew up the valley to a point perpendicular to the guerilla's camp and inserted twelve Navy Seals. The drop was about three miles from the guerilla camp to minimize the chance of being heard or seen. The element of surprise would be critical to the success of the operation.

As midnight approached, the Seals equipped with LED headlamps and night vision goggles, hiked up over the ridge and descended 1500 vertical feet through the thick forest. They paused roughly 300 yards from the target. With their night vision goggles they could plainly see the guerillas fire. They stowed their unnecessary gear, checked their weapons, and began a slow quiet advance toward the guerillas camp. They stopped just short of the camp and each camouflaged Seal took up a position behind a tree forming a semi-circle around the camp.

There was one guard standing next to a tent, the rest of the men were zipped up in their sleeping bags sleeping. The Seal Team Leader, Capt. Brown, motioned to the others that he would take out the guard while they attack the men in the sleeping bags. Capt. Brown raised his silencer equipped rifle and fired at the guard striking him in the head and killing him instantly. Simultaneously, the rest of the Seals moved in and shot and killed the remaining guerillas.

Capt. Brown ordered the Seal team to check the tent and sweep the area while he checked the bodies. He checked several bodies until he found what he was looking for. The body of Jack Cody with a bullet wound to the chest and head. With the mission complete, he radioed the base for extraction, and to report that the mission was successful, Jack Cody was dead.

President Adams was meeting with the Secretary of Defense and the Joint Chiefs at the Pentagon to review the status of the final assault.

"Mr. President, we are making extremely good progress on all fronts. We should have things wrapped up militarily by the end of the month," said General Tillman

"That's great news. Faith and fanaticism is no match for science and reason. Just as we have defeated the religion of Marx, we will defeat the religion of the prophets," responded an ecstatic President.

The General continued with details of the fighting in the Middle East when the commander of North American forces interrupted him.

"My apologies for interrupting Sir, but the President said he wanted to be notified immediately of any further developments with regard to the guerilla leader Jack Cody."

"Yes, quite all right Colonel. Please continue," replied the President.

"Yes Sir. I am pleased to report that a Special Forces team led by Capt. William Brown, located, surrounded, and destroyed the mountain camp of the theist guerillas at 2:00 AM Eastern Standard Time. Due to the element of surprise, and superior night vision technology, the guerillas were all killed with no Special Forces casualties. We have a positive identification on the guerilla leader Jack Cody, who was killed as he attempted to return fire."

"Now that is wonderful news. The last thing we need is to have to fight a guerilla war here at home. Well-done Colonel, tell Capt. Brown thank you for a job well done."

"Yes Sir."

Now that the only real domestic threat to materialize since the start of The Unity Project had been eliminated, the remaining operations would be able to move forward without further complications.

Camp Enlightenment

By first light, Alpha Company had already surrounded the God First Baptist Theological Seminary north of Little Rock, Arkansas. In what was to be an often-repeated scene, they surrounded the seminary grounds, and incrementally tightened the perimeter until they made their final move into the seminary buildings. This perimeter approach decreased the likelihood that any seminarians would be able to escape though the perimeter line. The seminarians that did try to escape were quickly subdued and put into waiting buses.

The troops burst through the front door of the seminary dormitory, and moved quickly into the rooms of the sleeping seminarians. They kicked the doors open and screamed at the sleepy students to get up and get dressed.

"Let's go! Move!" shouted one of the soldiers.

"You might want to move a little faster!" yelled another soldier.

The raid on the God First seminary resulted in the capture of 125 subversive seminarians. As the troops moved in and began handcuffing the students one of the seminarians spoke up, "Why are you here? Where are you taking us?" he asked.

"You will be taken to Camp Enlightenment for re-education," replied the soldier.

"But we don't want to be re-educated. We're getting a good Christian education here. We believe in the glory of God and Jesus Christ. We don't want to change our beliefs."

"You have violated the law, and have to be rationalized. Now get in line with the others."

The seminarians were lined up, loaded into waiting buses, and taken to Camp Enlightenment a few miles east of Rogers, Arkansas. The 1500-acre camp was one of several re-education camps that had been converted from Christian youth camps and retreats, and reconfigured to hold theist prisoners. Some of the larger seminaries captured by secularist forces, were converted to state universities, and the theological curriculum replaced with science and engineering programs.

The buses arrived at the gates of Camp Enlightenment, and were greeted by armed military police. A tall chain linked fence topped off with razor wire surrounded the camp. The buses were stopped and the guards made a quick inspection of the buses and their contents. Once the inspection was completed the gate was opened, and the buses were allowed to enter the compound. The winding road cut through rolling hills and forest. There were no signs of buildings or people anywhere. Eventually the buses reached a clearing, and entered the main compound. The compound consisted of several houses, three buildings that looked like barracks, a large building that looked like a lodge, and several other small buildings that looked like maintenance and storage sheds. This was to be the new home for the captured seminarians.

The buses came to a stop in front of the camp headquarters building where they were greeted by more armed military police and the camp's commandant. The prisoners were ordered to get off the buses, and form a line three deep. Once the lines were formed the camp's commanding officer addressed the prisoners.

"Welcome to Camp Enlightenment. We are delighted you have joined us on your journey into the world of knowledge and reason. Our purpose at Camp Enlightenment is to improve your mental and physical fitness, so that you can be returned to society as better and more productive citizens. You will remain with us until you have been rehabilitated and have passed the final examination. Upon successful completion of the final examination you will be released. The rules are simple, follow the rules and you will be rewarded, violate the rules and there will be serious consequences. From here, you will be taken to your rooms where you will be provided with uniforms. Then you will meet in the main auditorium for initiation and an introduction to the camp and its rules."

He then turned to his Sergeant, who was standing next to him and said, "This is Sgt. Wilson. Sgt. Wilson will be your instructor during your stay with us. Sergeant, they're all yours."

"Yes Sir," replied the Sergeant.

The Sergeant stepped forward to address the prisoners. Sgt. Wilson was a Marine drill sergeant. Tall, muscular and trim, impeccably dressed, with a Marine high and tight hair cut, shaved on both sides with a crew cut on top, he was a formidable figure. In a forceful voice the sergeant began to address the prisoners.

"My name is Sgt. Wilson. I will be your drill instructor during your stay with us. You will obey all orders. You must do everything you are told to do quickly and without question. The training here is tough. We expect nothing less than your very best effort at all times. Do you understand?

There was a tepid response from the prisoners. The sergeant barked back, "I did not hear a Yes Sir, Sgt. Wilson. Now, do you understand?" This time the prisoners responded with a hearty, "Yes Sir, Sgt. Wilson." Temporarily satisfied Sgt. Wilson continued.

"You are here to be rehabilitated. This includes the cleansing of your minds of irrational thoughts. Therefore, you will be referred to as scrubs until you have completed your reconditioning. Upon successful completion of your final examination, you will be referred to as citizens and released. Now, give me one line, single file. We will march to the barracks for your room assignments and uniforms."

Scrubs were only identified by a unique Identification Number, and were referred to as Scrub 456897 or Scrub 279413 by both the guards and the prisoners. Proper names were not permitted. The bright orange prison uniforms had the scrub's Identification Number printed across the front and back of the shirt.

Each prisoner was fitted with two indestructible non-removable wristbands one primary, one secondary for backup, placed on each arm. The wristbands could only be removed by transmitting a computer generated encrypted code to the receiver on the wristband, making it virtually impossible to remove. The wristbands had two purposes; tracking and punishment. The wristbands could be activated to induce a severe electric shock remotely or by the guards. The electric shock was non-fatal but painful enough to disable or punish a prisoner.

For tracking, the wristbands had an embedded Global Positioning System (GPS) locator, and a Radio Frequency Identification (RFID) tag. The whole camp was filled with sensors, which allowed the identification and tracking of the prisoners anywhere in the compound. Every room in the compound was equipped with a camera, which had a built-in microphone. With the wristbands and cameras, every action, every movement, and every conversation could be monitored from the camp's central monitoring control room. The guards knew the prisoners location, and what they were doing at all times. If one of the prisoners did manage to escape they could be tracked anywhere in the world.

The compound's tracking system was part of a larger system that allowed the government to track dissidents anywhere in the country, or the world. The process started by issuing each prisoner a unique ID number. The prisoner then would be assigned a room number, which would be tied to a building number, a camp number, a state number, and finally a country number. A file would be built that would contain all the known information about the prisoner. To determine a prisoner's location and personal information the only thing that was needed was the prisoner's Identification Number.

The first element in the re-education program consisted of confession and the exposure and renunciation of past and present evil. The past and present evil was a belief in false gods and the relinquishing of the mind to faith rather than reason. Confession and renunciation was followed by re-education, which consisted of the remaking of a person in the rationalist image. In the rationalist mind there is no room for false beliefs or superstitious thinking. Rationality was reality based correct thinking, whereas irrational belief was identical with the psychiatric characterization of a delusion. The re-education program used a series of pressures and appeals including, intellectual, emotional, and physical conditioning, aimed at the socialization of reason and the teaching of reality. Reality is how things actually are, in contrast with their mere appearances. Appearance has to do with how things seem to a particular perceiver or group of perceivers, but appearance does not determine reality.

The program was designed to stifle dissent by first defining religious belief as deviant behavior and causing overwhelming feelings of guilt in the prisoner, this was followed by psychological conditioning that rewarded newfound devotion to the principles of logic and reason. The prisoners were conditioned to accept, and eventually promote the secularist Technocratic regime, and the ideals of pure rational thought.

As the prisoners arrived at the camp they were processed. The processing of prisoners was a five-step process. First, the prisoners were forced to write a biography and a confession of their crimes against the state, a confession in which they would be continuously cross-examined. Second, the prisoner must recognize and admit to the nature of their counterrevolutionary conduct as an enemy of the state. They must also criticize their abhorrent behavior and past conduct. Third, the prisoner must completely submit to the state and the prison authority to demonstrate their subservience, and loyalty to the government. Fourth, he or she must demonstrate their loyalty to the state by spying and informing on other inmates in the prison. Fifth, the prisoner acquires redemption – a new consciousness based on logic and reason – through hard labor and study during their term as a prisoner.

The daily routine was both strenuous and challenging and left little time for the prisoner's minds to wander. The prisoners would arise at sunrise and begin the day with calisthenics and a three mile run. This would be followed by an indoctrination session, and then breakfast. The indoctrination sessions included classes on truth, reason, evidence, logical and rational thought, and scientific method. Breakfast was followed by four hours of hard labor, which generally included maintaining the facilities, building new structures and roads, or tending to crops. At noon there was a one-hour lunch break followed by four more hours of labor. The day would end with cleanup and dinner, followed by a nightly indoctrination session, which included a heavy dose of mathematics. Following the evening indoctrination session the prisoners would prepare for bed, sleep eight hours, and then start the routine all over again the next day.

Theists that could not be reconditioned at the re-education camps were placed in psychiatric hospitals for additional psychological treatment. The Technocrats considered these people to be mentally ill. Those that still believed in angels, gods, souls, satin, demons, spirits, and other irrational beliefs would fall under the general classification of suffering from mania fanatica, which is a form of insanity characterized by a morbid state of religious feeling. Mania is a form of insanity in which a person is subject to hallucinations or illusions accompanied by a high state of general mental excitement, sometimes amounting to fury. These people are impressed with the reality of events like the resurrection, which have never occurred, and of things like gods, which do not exist. They also suffered from delusions, which are erroneous beliefs that are held in the face of evidence to the contrary, and are obviously contrary to fact.

Many of the people the Technocrats considered to be too far gone for re-education converted to religion to find answers to deep-seated emotional problems and mental instabilities. Large numbers of theists that were classified as mentally ill suffered from auditory and visual hallucinations, which are symptoms of schizophrenia. These people insisted they had heard the word of God, or had spoken to God or one of his messengers. In some cases the Virgin Mary or God had appeared before them. Those that could not be reconditioned could expect a long stay in a psychiatric hospital. According to the Technocratic worldview, the deranged theists must be isolated in order to protect normal society and maintain social order.

The Battle for the Middle East

With the fall of Ukraine, Kazakhstan, Uzbekistan, and Turkmenistan, allied forces were on the borders of the last Islamic Front nations of Iran, Iraq, Saudi Arabia, Egypt, Libya, and Sudan. Since religious influence in the remaining parts of sub-Saharan Africa was already almost non-existent, all that was needed for victory was to cleanse the Islamic Front nations and finish destroying the remaining holy sites. The secularist forces had already begun positioning their troops for the final assault.

With the secularist forces making rapid progress the Council of Elders met again to discuss their strategy for slowing the allied advance. The Archbishop began the meeting.

"I'm afraid I have bad news to report. Today I learned that our top agent, and greatest hope for intelligence on troop and supply movements, Angela Kibble is dead. She succumbed to the evil influences of the godless ones."

The Council members' faces showed their disbelief and disappointment.

"We all mourn her loss. She was a faithful servant of God and made substantial contributions to the cause," said Elijah.

"Let us please have a moment of silence for Angela Kibble, our bold angel," said Nicholas.

After a moment of silence Nicholas continued, "I am afraid there is more bad news. The secularists are moving rapidly to the south. The resistance in Turkey and the former Soviet states has collapsed.

We are currently massing forces near the borders of the Islamic Front Nations, and will continue to fight to the death. The infidels will run into a wall of flame. God willing, we will destroy them."

"If we are going to have any chance of wining this war we can't let the infidels take control of the Islamic Front states," said Mustafa.

"The numbers don't look good. This wall of flame you talk about will be more like sheep for slaughter," said Surya.

Even though Surya was a Hindu and a firm believer in religious freedom, he was also a mathematician and a realist. He knew that the probability of success was close to zero and in his own mind knew that the fight was over. He had felt left out from the beginning, and he knew that his only chance for survival would be to change his identity and flee to a neutral country.

"We have to complete the formation of the guerilla forces and prepare for a long drawn out guerilla war if we have any hope of defeating the crusaders," said Mustafa.

The disagreement between Nicholas and Mustafa continued as Nicholas countered, "We need all available forces on the front lines. If we fail to stop them at the borders of the Islamic Front Nations, the war will be over. Their technology is too great to win a guerilla war. They can see through the ground, they can see through walls, the accuracy of their weapons is unparalleled. We must inflict heavy causalities now. They must pay in blood or they will not stop."

Clearly agitated, with the volume of his voice increasing, Mustafa fired back, "Direct confrontation with the infidels is doomed to fail. If all our soldiers are killed or captured the war will end, there will be no soldiers left to continue the fight."

Elijah, who had been listening intently, finally intervened, "We are obviously not all going to agree on the final tactics of the war. I recommend that we take a split approach. We allocate a sizable force to the northern front to slow down the godless ones and we move the remaining forces to strategic positions within the Islamic front nations. There we can form guerilla units to continue attacks."

"I agree that a split approach is the only chance we have to continue the fight," said Surya.

"The split force approach is a reasonable compromise," said Nicholas.

"There is nothing to gain from a direct confrontation with an overwhelming force. It will only serve to deplete our soldiers. I cannot support a split force approach," said Mustafa.

"Since the majority of the Council supports the split force approach, this is what we shall do," said Nicholas.

As the meeting ended, there was a general sense that further resistance was futile. It was only a matter of time before the technology of the western powers would overwhelm the theist forces. Mustafa was angry and upset that Nicholas was willing to sacrifice thousands of theist fighters in what would certainly be a devastating defeat. He truly believed that a prolonged guerilla war was the theist's only hope against the crushing power of the western crusaders.

Later that evening, the Archbishop arrived back in Alexandria, Egypt. He was on his way to one of the Council's safe houses when there was a terrible explosion. A powerful bomb tore through the motorcade of the Archbishop, killing him and his bodyguards instantly. The explosion gouged a crater in the street 25 feet wide and 10 feet deep and shattered windows and twisted the metal window frames of nearby buildings.

The news of the death of his friend Nicholas saddened Elijah greatly. Although they had their share of disagreements, he respected the Archbishop and considered him a great man. As he contemplated the death of the Archbishop, he had an uneasy feeling that his death had to be the work of Mustafa. No one else could have known about the movements of the Council members and had the means to carry out such a heinous act. With the death of Nicholas, he now feared for his own life, and decided it was better to live and fight another day. He decided that Africa, with its vast areas of undeveloped land, would be the best place to hide. He believed that as long as there were some remaining theists and the sacred texts were safe, eventually the great religions of the world would return to their past glory.

With the head of the Council of Elders dead, and Surya and Elijah fleeing for safety, it was left to Mustafa to finish the fight. There was no longer a cohesive command structure. The individual theist armies were now isolated and would have to be led by local commanders. Even though the theist leadership was now in disarray, Mustafa had no problem being a martyr for Allah.

The Battle of Ideas

While the battle for the Middle East was getting underway, the Commander and the Librarian were having another one of their weekly meetings.

"Well Professor, our forces have made rapid progress and are now moving into the last of the rogue Islamic states," said the Commander.

"It may have been easy up to now, but there you will face the stiffest resistance. This is the holy land of the true believers," replied the Librarian.

"Soon they will be true believers of logic and reason. There will be nothing left of their primitive shrines."

"What you call primitive shrines is part of their existence, part of their reason for living."

"How can a highly educated man with your vast knowledge believe in such folly?"

"I have believed since I was a small boy. I know no other way."

"How can one adhere to a philosophy of blind obedience, acceptance, and submission solely on the basis of what you have been taught or told without questioning the validity of this obedience? What about curiosity and free thought?"

"I felt no need to question the validity of my beliefs."

"There is no scientific evidence for any of the divine attributes normally associated with God."

"Which divine attributes are you referring to?" asked the Librarian.

"The divine attributes of omnipotence, omniscience, and omni-benevolence, do not exist anywhere in nature, and there is no evidence that they exist in the supernatural. If omnipotence is maximal power, in its true meaning, it would mean that God would have the power to do absolutely anything, including the logically impossible. The possessor of omnipotence could change the past, present, and future, and change the laws of nature at will. If God cannot do all these things and has limited power, then by definition there is no God."

"These things don't matter. We do not need to observe God's power to believe."

"After all the evidence against religion how can you still believe in an ancient mythology based on faith alone?"

"Doesn't all human belief and knowledge begin with faith?"

"Faith implies a belief for which there is no empirical evidence or rational proof. For a belief to claim the status of fact, it must be consistent and based on evidence. There is no evidence for God."

"That is the difference between the godless and the true believers. We don't require scientific evidence to believe. We believe because we have faith."

"Well professor, we may not agree on the need for evidence as a foundation of belief, but perhaps you would agree that the two great divides, which have resulted in the greatest sources of conflict in human civilization, are faith versus reason and individualism versus collectivism."

"Actually, I have not viewed things from that perspective before. I will have to think about these two concepts you call the two great divides."

"Very well professor, I will see you next week."

The Last Mission

The night before the mission Capt. Williams only had a short amount of free time. He missed Ashley terribly, and with the number of sorties increasing he didn't know when he would get another chance to call her. He tried to make a quick call and was fortunate to get through on the first try.

"Hey, Ashley, How are you?"

"Kyle! I miss you so much."

"I miss you too, I have a mission tomorrow and things are picking up around here, but it looks like the war will be over soon and I can come home."

"I hope so. I want you home."

"I can't wait to see you. Listen, I have to go. I just wanted to hear your voice. I love you."

"I love you too. Take care of yourself."

The next day, Capt. Williams completed his pre-flight check and climbed into the cockpit of his F-35EX Lightning. His pal Henry helped strap him into the cockpit and said, "Go get'em Cowboy, but keep an eye out."

"Thanks Gunner, see you in a couple hours."

While the load crew finished loading the weapons, Capt. Williams completed his final pre-taxi checks. The load crews are three person teams with a Master Sergeant, a Staff Sergeant, and a Senior Airman. The load crews handle the loading of munitions and weapons maintenance. Henry was the Crew Chief, and was responsible for the overall operation. The Staff Sergeant prepares the aircraft for loading, while the Senior Airman prepares munitions, and transports the missiles with a lift truck. For this mission, the team started by loading two 1,000-lb class air-to-surface GBU-32 Joint Direct Attack Munitions (JDAMs) in the main weapons bay, two heat-seeking AIM-9 Sidewinder short-range air-to-air missiles in the side weapons bays, and 1000 rounds of armor piercing ammunition for the M61A2 20-mm multi-barrel cannon. The M61A2 is capable of firing ammunition at a rate of 7,200 rounds per minute so a thousand rounds wouldn't last long. They finished by installing chaff and flares, which are part of the aircraft's defensive systems. Chaff are small bits of metal the aircraft dispenses in flight to confuse enemy radar. The flares are used as decoys for heat seeking missiles.

The load crew finished their job, and with all systems ready, Capt. Williams taxied out to the runway, and prepared to take off for his mission. He was cleared for take off and with a roar from his Pratt & Whitney's he was gone. At Mach 2.0 it didn't take him long to get to his target.

The mission for the day was a bombing run to take out an enemy command and control center in northern Iran. As the target came into site, Capt. Williams prepared to launch his weapon. Upon target acquisition he launched one of the JDAMs, flew past the target, performed a tight right turn, and flew back over the target to verify the destruction of the target. With the ability to hit a target with an accuracy of less than ten meters there wasn't much doubt that the target would be destroyed. The command center was totally destroyed. It was time to head back to the base.

As Capt. Williams entered Turkish airspace he received a message that an Army Ranger unit had been ambushed, was under heavy attack by insurgents, and needed close air support. After receiving the coordinates he headed for his next target. Capt. Williams arrived at the coordinates and did a fly over to get a better look at the situation. He could see what looked like a bunker and two tanks at the top of the valley.

The Rangers had been on an armed reconnaissance mission in a valley in the Kackar Mountains south of Rize, Turkey. There were still several insurgent units that would launch attacks against coalition forces then take refuge in the mountains. The plan was to position reconnaissance teams at strategic locations where they could establish observation posts to provide information on enemy movements, and direct air strikes against enemy forces. As the Rangers moved up the valley they came under intense mortar and small arms fire from both sides, and above their position. There were large rocks and trees that provided some cover from enemy fire. Before they could take cover a bullet hit Chief Warrant Officer Armstrong in the chest and knocked him down. Fortunately, he was wearing body armor and the other team members managed to pull him to safety behind some nearby rocks. Another bullet found Sgt. Carpenter, hitting him in the leg. He went down, but managed to roll behind some rocks to safety and began firing at the enemy positions. Finding themselves in a deadly crossfire with two of their teammates wounded and heavily outnumbered, they returned fire as Capt. Collins requested fire support.

After surveying the situation, Capt. Williams decided his first priority was to take out the bunker and the two tanks that were up high on the ridge. After completing his first fly over, he came back around, acquired his target, and launched his last JDAM. There was a tremendous explosion. He circled around for another run and saw that the tanks and the bunker had been destroyed. On the next pass he strafed the enemy forces that were attacking from the western side of the valley with the M61A2 cannon. The 20mm armor piercing bullets chewed up trees and insurgents alike. One more run to take out the insurgents on the eastern side of the valley and the Rangers would be home free. As Capt. Williams came in, he started firing his cannon, taking out the last remaining insurgents. Focused on taking out the enemy while avoiding the Ranger Team, he didn't see one of the insurgents setting up to fire a shoulder-launched surface-to-air missile. As he came in for his last pass, the insurgent fired the missile. The heat-seeking missile plowed into the F-35EX's jet engine and exploded.

With the plane disintegrating around him, Kyle reached down between his knees and grabbed the pull handle of his ejection seat. After a loud bang caused by the canopy separating, he was blasted into the air along with his seat. All the Rangers could do was watch as the plane broke up and crashed.

After Capt. Williams attack, there were only a handful of insurgents left alive. The Rangers were not about to let the one that fired the missile get out of the valley alive. They moved up the valley and engaged the remaining insurgents. There were chewed up trees and dead insurgents everywhere. They kept fighting until they reached the remains of the insurgent's camp. The fighting was over. All the insurgents had been killed. Capt. Collins and the Ranger team had been saved by the heroic acts of Capt. Williams.

True to the Ranger Creed, a Ranger will never leave a fallen comrade to fall into the hands of the enemy, the Ranger Team continued over the pass in an attempt to find the pilot. As they reached the top of the pass they spotted the wreckage of the downed aircraft. Upon reaching the plane they first checked the cockpit to see if the pilot was still in the plane. The ejection seat was gone and so was the pilot. It appeared that he had ejected from the plane before impact. They searched the area until one of the Rangers found a parachute. The pilot was still in his ejection seat, but it was too late. He had managed to eject from the plane, but the low altitude and high rate of speed were too much, as he slammed into the rocky slope of the mountain.

The next day, back at camp, Capt. Collins received word about the pilot who had saved their lives. Capt. Collins gathered the men together to tell them about the heroic pilot.

"I received some information this morning about the pilot who saved our asses up on the ridge yesterday. His name is Capt. Kyle Williams. He was based at Tyndall Air Force Base and had been flying missions out of Incirlik Air Force Base. He leaves behind a wife, his father and mother, and a brother," as a tear came to his eye he continued, "His wife is expecting their first baby. Today we pay tribute to Capt. Williams for his heroism, his extraordinary valor, and selfless courage. I'm sure that his wife and family are suffering terribly to have lost such a good man. I have written a letter to Mrs. Williams with our condolences and to let her know how much we appreciate her husband saving our lives, and his service to our country. I would like all of you to sign it."

Back in Florida, Ashley had just arrived home from work when she looked out the window and saw two airmen in service dress uniforms walking up the sidewalk. She felt a wave of grief rolling over her body, followed by a flood of uncontrollable tears. She knew why the airmen were there.

She opened the front door as the airmen reached the front porch.

"I am Master Sergeant Thompson and this is Staff Sergeant Leonard. We are representatives of the Air Force Chief of Staff from the 325th Fighter Wing at Tyndall Air Force Base. Are you Mrs. Ashley Williams?"

"Yes, I'm Mrs. Williams."

"On behalf of the Chief of Staff, United States Air Force, it is with deep regret that I inform you that your husband Capt. Kyle Williams died in Northern Turkey as a result of enemy fire while conducting a mission to extricate an Army Ranger unit under attack by enemy forces. While further details are unavailable at this time, you will receive a letter from your husband's commander, which will provide additional details. Additionally, the mortuary office at Tyndall will contact you regarding mortuary affairs. Again, on behalf of the Chief of Staff, please accept the Air Force's deepest condolences."

As the airmen spoke, all Ashley could do was cry. It was all like a bad dream.

"Is there anything we can do for you Mrs. Williams?" asked the Staff Sergeant.

Barely able to speak, all Ashley could say was, "Without Kyle, there is nothing."

The Master Sergeant handed her a card and said, "Here is my card. Please contact me if there is anything you need or if we can be of any assistance."

It was the worst feeling in the world. As the flood of tears continued, she felt like her very essence was being drained from her body, with the intense grief taking over her being. She closed the door, walked over to a chair and sat down. All she could do was cry and stare into blind space. She couldn't even imagine a life without Kyle.

The following week, the loss of Kyle had hit hard again as the funeral began. As the hearse entered the gravesite the airmen presented arms. The casket team removed the flag-draped coffin from the hearse, and carried it to the gravesite. The flag was placed over the coffin so the union blue was at the head and over the left shoulder of the Captain. The custom of a flag-draped coffin began during the Napoleonic Wars in the late 18th century, when a flag was used to cover the dead as they were taken from the battlefield on a caisson.

The funeral was to include a posthumous award of a Purple Heart, the Distinguished Flying Cross, and the Air Force Cross. The Air Force Chief of Staff read the citation. "We gather here today to pay tribute to the heroic efforts of Capt. Kyle Williams. In the frailty of our human existence, we find ourselves ill equipped to convey to one another the extremes of our emotions, for the peak of our love or the valleys of our feelings. I stand before you today in a humble attempt to assemble the words to honor a fallen hero. We gather today at this solemn event to honor a very special American hero, an airman who on the field of battle not only gave his life serving his nation, but also gave his life serving his fellow Americans. With these decorations, the highest decorations our Air Force can bestow, we humbly pay homage to his bravery, his selflessness, and his enduring sacrifice. This citation cannot compensate for the loss of a husband, brother, or son. Kyle stepped into the breach, and sacrificed himself so that others might live. On behalf of the United States Air Force and a grateful nation, we present this award as recognition of his extraordinary heroism and as a symbol of our deep gratitude of his loyal and honorable service."

"Captain Kyle Williams distinguished himself while participating in aerial flight as F-35-EX pilot, 325th Fighter Wing. Captain Williams personally prevented the probable overrun and total loss of an Army Ranger ground unit, killed one hundred and fifty enemy personnel, while simultaneously destroying two tanks as well as a bunker occupied by enemy forces. The outstanding heroism and selfless devotion to duty displayed by Captain Williams reflect great credit upon himself and the United States Air Force." He then presented the medals to Capt. Williams' wife Ashley.

Capt. Williams' commander performed the interment service, which was followed by a gun salute by seven airmen firing three volleys each. The gun salute came from an old battlefield custom. The two warring sides would cease hostilities to clear their dead from the battlefield. The firing of the three volleys meant that the dead had been properly cared for and the side was ready to resume the battle.

Two airmen marched up to the casket, removed the flag, and folded it into the symbolic tri-cornered shape. After Taps had been played, the flag was presented to Ashley. The airman stood at attention facing Ashley holding the folded flag waist high, with the straight edge facing her. He leaned toward Ashley and solemnly presented the flag to her and said, "On behalf of the President of the United States, the Department of the Air Force, and a grateful nation, we offer this flag for the faithful and dedicated service of Captain Kyle Williams."

As tears rolled down her cheeks, Ashley took the flag and held it to her chest over her heart. She rose from her chair and walked over and placed her hand on top of the casket and said, "Goodbye Kyle, I will always love you."

The funeral ended as a lone airman stood vigil over the casket. Despite overwhelming grief, somehow Ashley and Kyle's family would try to continue with their lives.

The Captain and the Teacher

The mission-planning meeting was just ending, when Sgt. Carpenter entered the tent with a message from CENTCOM that Archbishop Nicholas Milionis had just been assassinated in Alexandria, Egypt. They all knew that there would be a power struggle in the Council of Elders, and that the assassination of the Archbishop would severely weaken the theists.

Jake was worried that Maria's life might now be in danger, and left immediately after the meeting to find her. He returned to the Anatolia Café where he had last seen Maria. He entered the café and went to the makeshift classroom where he found Maria at her usual position in front of the class at the blackboard. Maria didn't notice him when he first entered the classroom. Jake stood motionless for a moment and watched Maria deliver her lesson. She was magnificent, so poised, and so smart, she had the children mesmerized. As she turned back to the class from the blackboard she noticed Jake standing in the back of the classroom. She stared at him for a moment; she could sense by the look on his face that something was wrong. She told the children to continue reading as she walked to the back of the room.

"Hello Maria."

"Hello Captain."

"I need to talk to you. Can we go outside?"

"Yes, but I cannot leave the children for long."

They walked out to the front of the café and Jake told her the news about her father.

"Maria, I'm afraid I have bad news. Last night, your father was assassinated in Alexandria, Egypt."

With a look of shock and disbelief, Maria cried out, "I don't believe you! That can't be true. I just spoke with him yesterday."

"I'm sorry Maria; we received the report this morning."

Maria started crying. As she pounded on Jake's shoulder she cried, "It can't be, it can't be." As the reality of the news sank in she just started crying and fell into Jake's arms. Maria cried on his shoulder as he held her and tried to comfort her.

"I'm so sorry, Maria," he said.

He let her cry then she looked up at him and asked, "How did it happen?"

"Enemies of your father blew up his motorcade as he was heading to a meeting in Alexandria, Egypt. He was killed instantly along with his driver and bodyguard."

"Who would want to kill my father?"

"We believe that there was a power struggle going on between the various theist factions over the prosecution of the war, and that the same people who tried to kill you are responsible for your father's death. We also believe that your life is in grave danger. I want you to come with me."

"But I can't leave the children," she pleaded.

"The opponents of your father have already tried to kill you once. You and all these beautiful children could have been killed. If you stay, you not only put yourself at risk, but you risk the lives of the children as well."

Maria was torn between leaving the children or staying and possibly risking their lives, but realized that the danger was real, and that she would have to leave. She told Jake to wait outside, and she would inform the children. The tearful Maria went back into the classroom to explain why she had to leave. As she tried to regain her composure she addressed the students.

"My dear children, I want you to know that I love all of you and for that reason I am going to have to leave you in the hands of another teacher. By my presence, I endanger all of you and I cannot allow that to happen. I want you all to remember that knowledge and learning are a life long adventure so please study hard in my absence. Please take care, and remember all that I have taught you. I hope to return soon."

As Maria walked down the aisle to the door many of the children began to weep and begged Maria to stay. She hugged several children on the way out and told them to be strong. She left the café and walked to where Jake was waiting, her eyes still wet from the many tears. Jake helped her into the Jeep and they left for the Ranger camp.

When Jake and Maria arrived back at camp, Sgt. Carpenter was there to greet them.

"Sgt. Carpenter this is Maria Milionis. She is the Archbishop's daughter," said Jake.

"My condolences on the passing of your father, ma'am," said Sgt. Carpenter.

"Thank you," replied Maria.

"Maria is going to be staying with us until we head back to Incirlik," said Jake.

"We already have a tent setup for her Sir," replied the Sergeant.

Later that night back in the relative safety of the Ranger camp, Jake took some food and water to Maria's tent. She was sitting on a rock gazing at the stars.

"Maria, I have brought you some food and water."

"Thank you Jake, but I am not hungry."

Jake put the tray of food and water on the ground next to the tent. After a few seconds of silence he said, "I know how hard it is to loose your father. My father died last year," said Jake as a tear came to his eye.

"I'm so sorry," said Maria.

Maria was surprised to see that such a tough and rugged man could be so sentimental. He seemed to have great empathy for others and had a sensitive side that Maria had not seen before. Jake was a soldier who could kill a man with his bare hands. But underneath his lethal appearance, he was a very gentle and caring man.

"Even though my father was almost eighty, and had a long and happy life, it was still sad when he died. It is always sad when people die, but no one lives forever."

"How do you handle death if you don't believe in a soul or an afterlife?" asked Maria.

"I believe that you have but one life to live. That is the life you enjoy while you are here on this wonderful planet. Humans are just organic matter with a marvelous brain. There are no afterlife, no soul, and no heaven," Jake replied.

"But if there is no better life in heaven, what is the purpose of life?"

"You have to live the one life you have to its fullest potential. You try to enjoy life, you try to lead a long, virtuous, and happy life, and you attempt to make the world a better place for future generations to enjoy."

"I know my father is in heaven now. He gave his life for Christ," said Maria.

She paused for a minute and thought about others who would loose their friends and family because of the war. Then she asked,"Aren't you scared that you will be killed and never see your family and friends again?"

"I do not fear death. I will not know when I am dead. The suffering from death comes to those left behind, who have to cope with the loss. I knew when the war began that there could only be three outcomes. I would survive the war, go home a hero, and live a full and happy life. I would be wounded, go home a hero, and attempt to live a full and happy life. I would be killed in action, and go home a dead hero. It all depends on what hand fate deals me."

"I hope fate deals you a good hand Jake."

He smiled and said, "Fate led me to you Maria, so I have already been dealt a good hand."

Maria returned the smile. It was the first time he had ever seen her smile. She was even more beautiful when she smiled. It made Jake feel good that he could get a smile out of her, even as she grieved. He had to be up early the next morning so he said, "I have to hit the sack. If you need anything at all please let me know. Goodnight Maria."

"Goodnight Jake."

The next morning Jake met with Maria to tell her that the mission in Turkey was over and they were heading back to Incirlik Air Force Base to prepare for their next mission.

Incirlik was a very busy place. There was the roar of airplanes constantly taking off and landing, and there were trucks and troops that seemed to be in perpetual motion. Incirlik had become the central hub for the transfer of troops and supplies. As the soldiers came and left, they were provided with food, a cot, a warm safe place to rest and entertainment outside of the hostile war zones. For Jake, it was merely a place for a hot shower, some food, and a chance to replenish his supplies.

The day after their arrival at Incirlik, Jake had to ship out for his next mission. He went by to see Maria before he left.

"Maria, I have to go."

"They didn't give you much time to rest."

"A lot more time than in Ranger school."

"Jake, I can't thank you enough for all you have done for me. I have never met a man like you before. I feel so safe around you. I don't know how I am going to survive without you."

"You will do fine. You'll be safe here, and I'll be back in thirty days."

Maria put her hands around his muscular neck, pulled his head to hers and kissed him on the lips.

"Please take care of yourself. I want to see you again."

Grinning from ear-to-ear, and feeling energized from Maria's kiss Jake said, "That just gave me even more reason to make it back alive."

He picked up his gear, and still smiling he said, "Goodbye Maria, see you in thirty days!"

The Final Meeting

After many meetings for tea and discussion, the Commander and the Librarian had become close friends. Although they had many philosophical disagreements, they respected each other's knowledge and wisdom, and their commitment to their beliefs. They both hoped the war would end soon and they could get back to leading a normal life. Today's meeting began with the Librarian asking, "Thomas, I am curious, what satisfies you and makes your life complete if you have no spiritual fulfillment?"

"Being with my wife and children, the quest for knowledge, and the study of nature give me infinite pleasure," replied the Commander. He paused for a moment and continued, "You know Alex, I've been thinking, most of our discussions have been about history, philosophy and the war. I haven't even had a chance to ask you about your family."

"I know. There is always so much to talk about and so little time."

"What about your family Alex, where are they now?"

"I never had time to settle down and marry," as he smiled he said, "Although there was this one librarian that I dated for awhile. I should have married that girl." After a short pause he started again, "My parents have both passed away, and the last I heard my brother was running an import business in Hong Kong. What about you Thomas?"

"I'm married and have two wonderful children," he said as he got up, walked over to his desk and picked up a picture of his family. He brought the picture over to show the Librarian.

"This is my wife Susan, my son Dennis who is eight years old, and our little girl Suzie who is six, she's named after her mother."

"They look like a lovely family. You must miss them very much."

"Being in the military is difficult. I don't get to see them as often as I would like. Perhaps when the war is over, I will have more time for them and my studies."

Their discussion time had ended and it was time for the Librarian to return to his cell. As the Librarian stood up to leave the Commander said, "Alex, I would like to know more about your family and what life was like when you were growing up. Next time, can we talk about that instead of philosophy and war?"

"Yes Thomas, I would enjoy that very much."

Later that evening the Commander was summoned to the infirmary. He was told the Librarian was ill. The Commander entered the infirmary and found the Librarian lying in bed.

"Hello Thomas," the Librarian said in a weak voice.

"Hello Alex. What are you doing in here? You're supposed to be preparing for our next discussion."

"I'm afraid there may not be another discussion."

"There has to be. We haven't finished solving the great problems of mankind, besides you haven't told me where the sacred texts are."

"You must continue the quest for knowledge for me."

Thomas had a feeling that his friend Alex was dying. He took the Librarian's cross from his pocket, and placed it in the Librarian's feeble hand.

"Here is your cross my friend, I'm sorry I did not return it sooner."

The Librarian smiled and said, "If am I right, I will see you again my friend."

As a tear came to the Commander's eye he said, "Yes Alex, if you are right I will see you again."

The Librarian closed his eyes for the last time taking the location of the sacred texts with him to the grave.

The Final Battle

The allied command center was aglow with flat panel screens displaying everything from live video feeds from airborne drones to maps displaying enemy and allied troop locations and movements. General Anderson had been monitoring events and waiting for his troops to be in position for the final assault. As the General completed his analysis Captain Phillips approached him and said, "General Anderson, Sir, all of the field commanders have reported that they are in position and awaiting your command for the final assault."

"Very good, Captain," he replied. He paused for a moment then continued, "This is certainly an ironic ending."

"How's that Sir?" asked the Captain.

"The three monotheistic religions all believe that Jerusalem would be the site of Armageddon, the final battle between good and evil before Judgment Day. For the Jews, the long awaited Messiah will return to become the king of Israel and high priest of a new temple on the Temple Mount. For the Christians, Jesus Christ will return to Earth and from the Temple Mount save the faithful and begin a new millennial reign. And for the Muslims, Jesus will return as a Muslim prophet and defeat the antichrist Dajal, the Ka'bah will be transported to Jerusalem, where Allah's final judgment of humanity, is preceded by the end of the world."

"They're right about one thing Sir; the end of days has arrived for the theists," replied the Captain.

"Thousands of years of history will be erased. Sadly, the theists leave us no choice," said the General. He paused once again and continued, "Put me through to the field commanders."

"Yes Sir!" replied the Captain.

The final battle against the Islamic Front Nations had begun. Shortly before the sea borne landings, a heavy naval and air bombardment destroyed most of the opposing forces. At sunrise the allied forces invaded from the Mediterranean Sea in the north, while a naval attack and amphibious landing was occurring from the Arabian Sea in the south. Naval forces in the Mediterranean Sea attacked Libya, Egypt, Jordan, and Syria. Ground forces based in Turkey moved into Iran, Iraq, and Syria. By nightfall the allied forces had moved inland 100 kilometers and secured the beachheads. In the Far East, the Philippines had already been cleansed and China and Japan had moved into Malaysia and Indonesia and were finishing clean-up operations.

Still believing their gods would save them the theists retreated to their remaining holy sites. In Iraq, the destruction of Islam's remaining holy sites was already well underway. Karbala, in central Iraq, is the site of the tomb of the Shi'a Muslim saint Hussein. It is second only to Mecca in the number of Shiite pilgrims that visit the holy sites. The Imam al-Hussein shrine was destroyed by the Wahhabis in 1801 but was rebuilt. This time, its destruction would be final.

The gold domed mosque of Imam Ali bin Abi Talib – named after the slain cousin and son-in-law of Islam's Prophet Muhammad – was built in 977 AD in Najaf, a city regarded by Shi'a Muslims as the faith's third holiest city in the world after Mecca and Medina in Saudi Arabia. The Shi'a Muslims consider Imam Ali to be their founder and first Imam. Only Mecca and Medina received more pilgrims. The site of the tomb of Imam Ali in Najaf, Iraq was also destroyed by air strikes along with the thousands of radicals that had been waging the terror war against western civilization.

Medina is considered to be the city of the Prophet Muhammad by the Muslim faithful. Its importance as a religious site is due to the presence of the Masjid al Nabawi or Mosque of the Prophet, which was built on the site of Muhammad's home and where he is buried. Many of the devout Muslims from other lands aspire to be buried there, to rise from the dead with Imam Ali on Judgment Day. Judgment Day had arrived, but no one was rising from the dead.

The remaining fighters of the Islamic Front Army had all retreated to Mecca for their final stand. They prayed that Allah would strike down the infidels and save them all. Mecca was the holiest site of Islam. For Muslims, a pilgrimage to Mecca is required as one of the Five Pillars of the faith. The focal point of Mecca is the Ka'bah, the "House of God" believed by Muslims to have been built by Abraham and his son Ishmael. Mecca is also the home of the al-Masjid al-Haram, or 'The Sacred Mosque,' which is for Muslims the holiest mosque on earth. The 1979 occupation of the Sacred Mosque by Muslim extremists had once before shaken the foundations of Islam. Since then thousands have died from stampedes and riots during the Hajj, which is the great pilgrimage to Mecca. The destruction of the Ka'bah and the Sacred Mosque in Mecca would insure the end of Islam.

The Temple Mount, in the old city of Jerusalem, the site of conflict between Jews and Muslims for centuries was destroyed. To the secularists, the Temple Mount symbolized all that was wrong with religion. It is the holiest site of Christianity and Judaism, and the third holiest site of Islam. Despite its status as a holy site, the reasons for this status are different for each of the three monotheistic religions. To the secularists it is home to primitive rituals and beliefs, and a source of contention and conflict between Christianity, Islam, Judaism, and countless other sects.

The Al Aqsa mosque is part of the complex of religious buildings in Jerusalem known as the Al-Haram al-Sharif or the Noble Sanctuary to Muslims, and the Temple Mount to Jews. The Al Aqsa mosque is on the site where Muslims believe Muhammad ascended to heaven. The Muslims claim that the Western Wall is part of the Al Burak wall, which is part of the Al Aqsa mosque, and belongs to Muslims, and Jews have no rights there. They believe it is their religious property that was taken from them by force, and God willing, they will take it back one day. Since the wall surrounding the mosque is the Western Wall venerated by Jews, this had been a major source of friction. There have been times when enraged Muslims worshipping at the mosque have hurled stones at the Jews praying below at the base of the Western Wall.

The Dome of the Rock is an Islamic shrine in Jerusalem. It was the site of the first and second Jewish Temples. According to Jewish tradition, the rock was the altar upon which Abraham prepared to sacrifice Isaac; Islamic tradition holds that it was Abraham's first son, Ishmael, the father of the Arabic people, whom Abraham was called upon to sacrifice. Muslims believe that the shrine is built around the rock where the prophet Muhammad ascended to heaven.

Also destroyed were the Church of the Holy Sepulcher in Jerusalem, considered to be Christianity's holiest place, and the Church of the Nativity in Bethlehem. Christians believe that the Church of the Holy Sepulcher covers the traditional site of the Jesus crucifixion-resurrection mythology, and that the Church of the Nativity is the place where the mythical Jesus was born.

Christians and Jews believe that the Jews are the only people with a right to the land of Israel as defined by scripture and that all others should leave. The destruction of the holy sites would finally remove the major points of contention between the three major religions. The old arguments of the past over the ownership of the sacred sites based on fables and mythology would no longer matter. Without religion as a basis for conflict, the centuries of war in the Middle East could finally come to an end.

The final destruction of Islam's holiest sites completely demoralized the remaining adherents. Mecca, Medina, and Riyadh, Saudi Arabia fell to coalition forces on June 21, 2076 and the allied leaders called upon the remaining Islamic countries to surrender unconditionally. The remaining Islamic Front nations surrendered on July 1, 2076. To complete the final phase of the Unity Project coalition forces had to round up and tag the remaining fanatical insurgents, send in the CESDUs to cleanse the remaining religious sites, confiscate religious books and icons, establish the re-education camps, and cleanse the minds of the theists.

Feeling abandoned and convinced that no God would save them, many of the remaining adherents sank into the depths of despair. Everything they had ever believed in had proved to be wrong. Their faith in God shattered as the foundations of their faith were erased from the face of the earth. There was no longer any doubt of the superiority of science and technology over faith.

For others, faith in the eventual coming of a savior and redemption continued. While their faith remained strong, they had no choice but to hide their beliefs or face time in the re-education camps. Most of the remaining religious leaders created new identities and went into hiding. Many still believed that one day the great religions of the world would rise from the ashes.

In America, the destruction of religious structures was nearly complete. Book burnings continued as additional copies of religious texts were found. The last of the old seminaries was converted to a state university and the re-education camps were operating with great efficiency. There were sporadic protests by small groups of religious fanatics, but the protesters were quickly arrested and sent to the re-education camps. The Unity Project was now nearly complete. Weary of war and conflict, America and the rest of the world looked forward to a new era of peace and harmony.

At the end of July, after combat operations had ended, and cleanup operations in America were winding down, the President addressed the nation and the world.

"Citizens of the world and my fellow Americans, we have been through a long and difficult struggle. Because of our bold action to eliminate the scourge of primitive belief systems and ethnic and racial divisions, future generations will come to know the true meaning of peace and tranquility. With the directed energy of millions of minds that have heretofore been wasted on primitive mythologies, the world will see the dawning of a new era of scientific achievement and unprecedented prosperity. I want to personally thank everyone whose courage and sacrifice have made this miraculous achievement possible. We will never forget those who died so that future generations can live in peace and harmony in a secure world. We still have more work to do. We must keep looking forward while healing the wounds of the past, we must continue to promote the principles of truth and reason, we must insure that all the citizens of the world are educated, and we must reduce poverty and bring prosperity to all nations. With the hard work and support of the global community, I know we can achieve these noble goals. Thank you and good night."

The Last Days

After the war, Commander Baker retired as planned. He had spent the years following the end of the war writing a comprehensive history of the War of Unification, as it was now called. During his writing he often thought about his friend the Librarian and how he wished he was still alive to discuss history, philosophy, and his interpretation of the war.

While writing, he liked to read his work verbally. Reading verbally helped him analyze the flow and consistency of the text. He would often read to his son, who was never shy about adding his comments. One night, the Commander was in his study working on his book when his son Dennis entered the room.

"Are you still working on that book?" asked Dennis.

"Yes, but believe it or not, I am almost done," replied the Commander.

"That's great, maybe now we can finally start playing sports again."

"I would enjoy that as well. I am finishing the final section called The Last Days. May I read it to you?"

"Sure, I would like to hear it, especially if it is the ending."

The Commander began reading, "The theists saw a world dominated by a tyrannical evil power of boundless destruction. As the tyranny of the evil power became ever stronger and its victims suffered ever greater under the weight of the oppressor, the Saints of God believed they would rise up and extinguish the suffering and would in turn inherit the earth. This would be the culmination of history. They had seen the signs, which marked the beginning of the last days and faithfully believed the prophecy that their savior would come and save them all. Their savior never arrived. Doomed by faith in a false prophecy, their end came swiftly."

"For a brief moment they saw what the future could hold. For a brief moment in time all the religions were unified in a common struggle for survival. Unity had finally been achieved. There existed a common goal, a common belief, and a common need. Yet without a unifying force, they were natural enemies, destined to become an aberration in history."

"The rationalist alliance was unified by a common commitment to world unification, and to rid the world of two thousand years of primitive conflict and warfare. The alliance did not wait for a savior, nor did they believe in prophecy. They believed in themselves and their cause. They believed in their mission to build a better world, free of ignorance and hate, and free of poverty and war. They believed that humans control their own destiny, not the hand of a false god."

"And that is the end. What do you think?" asked the Commander.

"That was very good father. Those were interesting times."

"It was a different world back then."

"What was it like before the War of Unification?"

"Well son, there was great turmoil and chaos in the world. There were many wars going on, all in the name of religion. Islamic terrorists were conducting suicide-bombing missions designed to kill innocent men, women, and children. They were cutting the heads of Americans and others like they were sheep for slaughter. This was all done in the name of their false god, Allah. The Christians and Muslims where killing each other on every continent. The Hindus and the Sikhs and the Hindus and the Muslims were killing each other in India. The Jews and the Islamic Palestinians were at war in the Middle East. The theist barbarians were attempting to take over the world, and divide it into religions regions, states, and theocracies. Religious violence and the attempt to divide the world into religious fiefdoms resulted in the War of Unification."

"Could religion ever come back again?" his son asked.

"The chances are minimal, now that most humans have overcome their superstitions and fear of the unknown. We can only hope that the evils of religious and ethnic conflict have been eliminated, and that the barbarism of primitive man will never rise again."

"What about the legend that the sacred texts still exist?"

"That's just what it is son, a legend. No one knows for sure. After the Librarian died and the war ended, there was an attempt to find the sacred texts, but they were never found. For the sake of humanity, hopefully they will never be found."

www.ingramcontent.com/pod-product-compliance
Lightning Source LLC
Chambersburg PA
CBHW060806120626
46557CB00001B/107